"You have always been safe from me, Spence. You know that, don't you?" She tossed the ice cream scoop and it landed with a plop in the de-icer bag. "I'm not on the hunt for a husband."

"You don't automatically want a sparkling diamond ring?"

"I'm the exception to that rule." She watched his shoulders visibly relax. Poor Spence. He believed that. He must have a poor opinion of women and marriage. "When I decide to hunt for a husband, I'll set my sights on a quality man."

"Are you suggesting I'm not?" He was grinning wide enough to show that hint of a dimple again.

She forgot to feel uncomfortable around him when he smiled like that. "I'm just saying that I'm not looking right now. But as far as quality goes, you're a good man, Spence. You shouldn't work so hard to hide it."

JILLIAN HART

grew up on her family's homestead, where she helped raise cattle, rode horses and scribbled stories in her spare time. After earning her English degree from Whitman College, she worked in travel and advertising before selling her first novel. When Jillian isn't working on her next story, she can be found puttering in her rose garden, curled up with a good book or spending quiet evenings at home with her family.

New York Times Bestselling Author

JILLIAN HART

His Holiday Heart

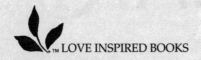

 ™ LOVE INSPIRED BOOKS

ISBN-13: 978-0-373-78793-7

HIS HOLIDAY HEART

Therefore, as the elect of God, holy and beloved,
put on tender mercies, kindness, humility,
meekness, long-suffering, bearing with one another,
and forgiving one another...but above all
these things put on love.

—*Colossians* 3:12–14

Chapter One

"I know your secret, mister."

Spence McKaslin jerked his attention away from the spreadsheets and frowned at his sister, Danielle. She was leaning against the doorjamb to his office with her arms crossed in front of her. Somehow she managed to look kindly and meddling all at once. He frowned. "What secret do you think you know? I don't have any secrets. I don't have time for any."

"Sure. I know you're a busy man." She laughed. A loving soul, she always had a smile for everyone these days, especially since her hardship at home was over. Her wedding ring sparkled as she shook her head at him with utmost disapproval. Mischief flashed in her dark eyes, and she gave an eye roll. "You can't fool me, big brother. I'm on to you."

"Wow, I'm really worried." What on earth was she talking about? he wondered. What did she think she knew? It had to be really good, considering the amusement on her face. He didn't approve of amusement.

Amusement had never helped him. He shoved his

chair back and moved a little. His muscles were stiff from sitting in the same position for the past hour or so.

Snow was falling harder outside his office's corner window, obscuring the buildings across the parking lot and disguising the pavement so it looked like a winter wonderland. He scowled. He didn't like wonderlands either. "Talk to me about something real. Something that matters. How's the traffic?"

She flashed him that glimmer of humor. "It's November, you know that, right? I heard that it's snowing. This morning it was sunny, and now there's a surprise winter storm advisory out there. The roads are a mess."

It was his turn for an eye roll. *This* is what he got for working with family. Family you couldn't choose, and they were impossible to order around. Harder to fire. He tried to hide his great affection for Danielle behind a bigger scowl. He had a reputation to protect. "I was asking about the store."

"I know." That stubborn cheerfulness didn't dim one iota. "Spence, you would be an incredibly handsome man if you would just put a smile on your face."

"Now you're sounding like Dorrie." Dorrie was his stepmom and Danielle's mom. "I'm not falling for that handsome line. I don't mind looking homely and disagreeable."

"Sure, *you* don't, but the rest of us have to look at you, brother dear." She gave him a wink, still lighthearted and apparently distracted from the topic of his secret.

Whew. He had only one secret and no one—repeat no one—knew about that. There were days when that secret was so secret that he almost couldn't remember it himself.

"We haven't had a customer for the last two hours."

Danielle gave him the look—the mom look she used on her kids. "I've counted down the tills, I'm turning over the sign and I'm going home."

Good thing he was immune to the mom look. "This is my store. We stay open until closing time."

"I'm driving home while I can still navigate the roads. I sent Kelly home, too."

"What?" That brought him to his feet. This was his store and Katherine, whom Danielle had replaced as his assistant manager, understood that. He and Dani were still figuring out how to work together. She was still new, but that didn't mean she could go usurping his authority. "Customers depend on us to be open."

"Customers are not going to be fighting through the snow to find us on Thanksgiving Eve." That smile faltered, and it was replaced by something worse—sympathy, maybe even pity. "I know you don't want to go home. I understand what it's like to unlock the door and step into an empty house. Remember when Jonas was in the Seattle clinic?"

"I remember." Remembering made his chest tangle up with a whole lot of feelings he had no interest in feeling. Jonas, his brother-in-law and Dani's husband, had been shot on a routine traffic stop a year and a half ago, and no one had thought he would recover from his traumatic brain injury. But he was coming along just fine. Grateful, Spence swallowed hard, managing to beat down every emotion. "Go home to your husband and kids. They're waiting for you. I'll close up here."

"I don't want you staying late." Her look turned to one of concern. "You're welcome to drop by for dinner. Jonas is cooking, and he's gotten pretty good. He's been watching cooking shows on television. I think he's doing homemade pizza tonight. It should be tasty."

Sure, he knew what she was doing, offering him a balm for his loneliness. He couldn't count the number of times he'd taken her up on it, and he liked the idea of having somewhere to be. He and Jonas could catch a sports show. There were the munchkins—his little niece and nephew—to play with. One thing he liked was Dani's kids.

But what if he had failed to distract her? What if she really had figured out his secret? Then there was no way he was going to put himself in close proximity to her so she could bring that secret out in the open. He hated to, but he forced out the words. "No, thanks. Maybe another night."

"Sure. Okay." Danielle took a step back, and that mischief returned to her eyes. She disappeared into her office for a few minutes, and the next time he saw her she was wearing a black wool coat and had her purse in hand.

"Drive safe," he called out, going back to his worrying spreadsheets.

"I will. Thanks." Danielle stopped at his door. "I should tell you that you're not alone in the store. Lucy came—"

"*Lucy?*" he interrupted. The spreadsheet numbers rolled right out of his head. His mind went blank. His lungs forgot to suck in air. "Lucy Chapin is here?"

"You don't have to say that like she's contagious with the bird flu. She's signing a shipment of her latest book because I asked her to," Danielle explained as if that was no big deal.

It *was* a big deal. His pulse began to thud in his ears. His palms went damp—a sure sign of panic. "Lucy is here right now?"

"She's in the break room. Are you all right, Spence? You've gone beet-red."

"Just my blood pressure." Or worse. And in that moment his worst suspicions about Danielle had come true. Not only did she know how he felt about Lucy Chapin but she was leaving him alone with her on purpose. There was no other explanation. "How did you know?"

"Careful observation." Danielle didn't even look apologetic as she turned on her heels. "I'm thinking she'll be done in a few minutes. The least you can do is thank her, and see if she needs anything else."

"You do it."

"Sorry. I've got to get home. Talking to her would do you good, Spence." She called over her shoulder and sauntered around the front counter. "Call me, and tell me how it goes."

He couldn't see anything other than red. Bright crimson splashed across his field of vision. He put his hands to his face. This was too much. How had she guessed? Danielle was good; he had to give her that. Somehow she had figured out he had a tiny, miniscule, barely nothing at all crush on Lucy Chapin.

Not that you could really even call it a crush. More like a dysfunction of his eyes, which made them always turn toward her whenever they were in the same room. That was all. Nothing more. Nothing serious.

He didn't believe in love. Not even a little bit. So he got up and closed the door. With any luck, Lucy would finish her signing and leave all on her own without a single word to him. Besides, it wasn't as if she liked him either. She'd always done her best to steer clear of him.

With any luck, she would avoid him, and his eyes wouldn't malfunction and glue to her pretty face and gentle smile. Comforted, he bowed his head over his profit ratios and tried to concentrate.

The phone rang. He snatched it up. "Corner Christian Books. How can I help you?"

"Spence?"

Wait. He knew that soft voice, as melodic as lark song. Every defensive shield he had went up around his heart. "Lucy?"

"I'm calling from the break room. Danielle said you were busy in your office, and I didn't—"

His ears stopped taking incoming information. There was just a haze of static as he digested what she'd said so far. She was calling him from the break room? He shook his head. That was something his younger sister Ava would do—the flaky sister. He adored Ava, but he didn't trust her with a set of keys to the store. "You're calling me when you're what, ten yards away?"

"Sure." She seemed unfazed by that or at least unable to see that her behavior was, well, quirky. "I didn't want to interrupt you."

"By knocking instead of calling?"

She was silent a moment, but when she spoke, her voice was still stubbornly meadowlarkish. "This is just a quick call. I've hauled the books back to the storeroom in the boxes, just like they came. I'll go out the back, and I'll be out of your way, but I wanted to make sure the alarm wasn't on. I don't have the best luck with alarms."

"No, I haven't set it yet."

"But Danielle locked up and turned off the store lights, and so I just wanted to make sure—" She must have felt she had to explain.

He was probably sounding terse again. Well, better that than vulnerable, right? He was grateful for the hard-won shields he'd learned to put up around his heart—around everything. "Fine. I understand. You're free to go."

"Great. Thanks." Surely he'd insulted her, but it didn't show in her voice. "Have a good evening. Bye."

The line went dead, but he couldn't seem to move. Even her voice had a strange effect on him. Her kind alto seemed to circle around in his head, and he wished for one second that he was a different kind of man— one who believed in true love and happy endings and all that make-believe stuff. Because if he could, then at least he wouldn't be alone. Instead of wishing he'd never see Lucy Chapin again; he would be hoping he could see her again. Talk to her. Take her out to dinner. But he wasn't that kind of a man.

He was the type of man who went back to his work. To his responsibilities. The store was his parents'. Some thought that meant an easy ride, since he'd walked into this job and his parents weren't about to find fault with him. But working for his folks meant something different to him. Commitment. Responsibility. Going beyond and doing all he possibly could. It was the least he could do for Dad and Dorrie. He disappointed a lot of people every day, but one thing he would never do was disappoint them.

The phone rang again. Good thing he'd stayed behind. He grabbed the receiver. "Corner Christian Books. How can I help you?"

"Spence?" said a familiar gentle voice. "It's me again. Lucy."

Lucy. He grimaced, fighting to keep his mind from going numb. His senses from going to static. To keep the steel around his heart.

"I can see you're not thrilled I bothered you again," she went on, apologetically but obviously not sorry enough to hang up and put him out of his misery. "Believe me, I called everyone else I know. The trouble is I don't know all that many people, at least anyone I can call during a blizzard to come get me."

"To come get you?" He swallowed hard, grateful his guards were still up. Now he just had to keep them there. "That sounds like car trouble. Won't it start? I'll call the auto club. I'll have someone here immediately."

"Oh, if only that was the problem. Then it would be easily solved."

"Then what's the problem?"

"The snowplow went by and buried my car. I can't get it out. I don't suppose you have a shovel I can borrow."

"A shovel?" He put a hand to his forehead and started rubbing as if he had a sudden, mammoth headache. "No. Sorry."

"Okay. Just thought I'd ask." She could see him across the parking lot. His forehead was still in his hand. There was no missing that grimace of his. She turned away, not wanting to see it. Not wanting to watch him when he thought he was alone. She tried to tell herself it didn't matter. Spence McKaslin was more like the abominable snowman whenever he was around her, which is why she stayed away from him whenever possible. She knew him only in passing; she hardly knew him at all. But she did know that he was very standoffish. She should give him a break and figure out someone to call—like a cab company.

"Sorry to bother you. Goodbye." She disconnected and pocketed her cell phone. The wind gusted, and she was shivering in her new goose down coat, which was supposed to keep her warm in minus twenty degrees. She was just a little cold. She clenched her jaw to keep her teeth from clacking together.

Her phone rang. She checked the screen. It was the bookstore. She unclenched her jaw enough to speak. "Spence?"

"Where are you?"

He sure didn't sound happy. She glanced across the parking lot, and the light in his office was out. Her teeth were chattering again. "I'm on the n-north side of the complex. I p-parked along the street."

"Why did you do that?"

Take a deep breath, Lucy. It wasn't his fault that he was the one man who could make her feel, well, less than adequate. "Because I had errands in a few other stores, and I didn't want to waste gas, so I walked."

"Why?"

"You've heard about the greenhouse effect? How about that walking increases cardiovascular health?"

Total silence.

Great. She took another breath and really wanted the phone call to end. No one—*no one*—made her more uncomfortable than Spence McKaslin. "Anyway, thanks. Bye."

"Wait." He barked out the word like an order.

That annoyed her, too. She didn't want to be annoyed, but it was almost a reflex when it came to Spence. He was a hard man to like.

"I'm not going to shovel you out with a wind chill of minus twenty and falling, but I will give you a ride home."

Oh, joy. Beware of getting what you pray for. She'd wanted help, but she hadn't wanted it in the form of Spence McKaslin. A grizzly bear would be a friendlier commuting buddy. If there was any simpler solution, she would take it hands down. But she'd been outside only a few minutes, and not a single soul had driven by. Everyone was gone from the other stores and shops in the shopping complex and along the opposite street, so she said the fateful words, "That would be great. Thank you."

Accepting his offer wasn't the most comfortable idea she'd had in awhile, but it beat standing out in an approaching blizzard.

"I'll be right there." He sounded so grim, he could have been accepting an appointment for five consecutive root canals. The line clicked off abruptly.

Her teeth were clacking together again, so she clenched her jaw. The wind cut through her layers of clothing, past her skin and went right into the hollow of her bones. Yikes, she was cold. But headlights flared to life at the back of the row of stores and swept around snowdrifts and parking curbs in her direction.

She was too cold to brace herself, as she always had to whenever she was in the vicinity of Mr. McKaslin. She had a short and unpleasant history with him—the unpleasant outweighed the short. When she'd moved from Portland to Bozeman, she joined a reader's group to get to know some people and because she loved reading. She had made many friends, Katherine McKaslin Munroe, who'd been the assistant manager but who was now on leave, her sisters Danielle, Ava, Aubrey, Lauren and Rebecca. She had heard about the Gray Stone Church from Katherine, joined and made a new circle of friends. But every time she stepped foot inside the bookstore or spotted him in church, Spence scowled at her, turned his back and acted as if she did not exist.

The ride home ought to be interesting. She wondered if he would even say two words to her. She lived a long way from town. Did she really want to be in Spence's presence the entire way?

His huge green truck skidded to a halt beside her. The door swung open. The dome light shone down on the big man, looking bigger in his thick winter coat, and seemed to emphasize his frown. He did not seem happy to see her.

He wasn't going to be happy when he found out where she lived. Maybe having him drive out all that way was too much. She could always stay in a downtown hotel. She stepped up into the truck not too clumsily, considering how she was nearly frozen solid. She collapsed on the seat and pulled the door shut, sprinkling large chunks of snow all over the pristine interior. "Sorry," she said.

He stared at her without acknowledging her apology. He would be totally handsome if he stopped scowling. He had wide set dark-blue eyes that would put a movie star to shame, high granite cheekbones and a straight blade of a nose. A mouth that might be bracketed by dimples, if he ever actually smiled. He had one of those strong square jaws that spoke of integrity and manliness.

"Where can I take you?" he asked in a baritone devoid of warmth or friendliness.

She felt colder in his truck with the heat blasting almost lukewarm than she'd felt outside in the minus degree windchill. Why did she want things to be different between her and Spence? She never could explain her feelings, why she felt sad whenever he behaved this way toward her. He wasn't the kind of man she even liked.

But he was a decent man. He was helping her when she really needed help. "Let's head toward the university."

"Sure." He put the truck in gear. "I know you're cold, but put on your seat belt."

That almost didn't come out sounding like an order.

Wow, this was going so much better than she expected. If only she wasn't board-stiff in the seat, she would be able to get the seat belt around the fluff of her inches thick coat.

Take a deep breath, Lucy, she instructed herself. Maybe the problem with Spence McKaslin was that he had always been a total stranger. So what if he had taken care to keep things this way. Maybe this was a God-given opportunity. Maybe her car was snowplowed under several feet of snow for a higher purpose.

She dropped her bag on the floor, latched the buckle and attempted to relax against the seat. The windows were fogged up and before Spence would drive an inch, he switched the heater to defrost and pulled a folded towel from beneath the seat to wipe the glass.

The way Spence leered at her out of the corner of his eye made her feel like a slacker.

"If I reach under my seat, will I find a nifty towel, too?" She asked, wanting to help out.

"No."

That made her wonder what he kept under the passenger seat. Something sensible, she figured, because this was Spence McKaslin—the man who she'd seen crack a smile once, but it had been short-lived and she had been way across the room from him. Definitely something practical, she decided. Probably an emergency tool kit or a first aid kit. It was unlike the mess of books she had beneath hers, which had slipped beneath the seat one by one after she'd left each of them on the floor.

"Here. If you don't mind." He folded the towel over to a dry side and handed it to her.

Talk about scintillating conversation. For once couldn't a handsome man—even a scowling, bad-tempered handsome man—look at her and say, "You look lovely, Lucy, even with a frozen nose and your eyelashes iced together"?

She took the towel from him. "Sure, I'd be happy to."

He grunted, nodded once and put the truck in gear. The vehicle rolled forward, and he expertly managed a huge slick of solid ice and turned onto the main road.

He remained silent as she wiped at the foggy glass. He didn't say, "This is great. We've never really had the chance to get to know one another, so let's do that now. How about a romantic dinner? Maybe some hot tea afterward in front of a roaring fireplace, and we can talk for hours."

No, he didn't say anything like that. He stared straight ahead as if he were pretending she wasn't seated right beside him. He didn't even sneak a look at her. She knew, because she was watching him. It was as if she didn't exist to him at all.

Bummer. She wished she could explain what it was about Spence that made her want to like him. It was just her romantic heart, she thought as she folded the towel a final time. The window was clear so she set the towel next to her bag instead of on the leather upholstery. She was a writer for a reason, mostly because this was her life—dull, staid and quiet. If she didn't have an imagination to spice it up, she'd be lethally bored.

But not even her imagination was strong enough to figure out how to turn Spence's silence into polite conversation.

So she contented herself with watching the windshield wipers swipe from side to side and the huge snowflakes evading them.

Chapter Two

S pence squinted through the snow on the window and couldn't believe his eyes. "This can't be right. You don't live in a hotel, do you?"

"No, but I live way out on Blackhawk Hill, and that's too far to ask you to drive."

"You should have asked me," he said. The shields were up around his heart, so he was certain he was immune to her incredible loveliness. Even with her hair wet from the snow and straggling against the sides of her face, she was breathtaking. Not that he wanted her to know that's what he thought. "I'm not leaving you here. I said I'd take you home, and I meant it."

"Did you hear the road report? Half the county roads are closed down. I should have left sooner, but I promised Danielle I would get those signed before your Thanksgiving week sale, and it's been one of those days. It's my fault, so you shouldn't be punished for offering to take me home."

That was a woman's logic for you. Spence scowled harder. He respected women and he liked them, but as the older brother of six sisters, he'd learned girls were a puzzle—and not logical in the slightest. "I'm taking you home where I know you're safe."

"Really? And here I thought you would be in a hurry to get rid of me." She said it with a smile, with understanding, as if she thought she knew why he always kept his distance.

She knew nothing. Nothing at all. All it took was one glance into her unguarded green eyes and his Adam's apple stuck in his throat and wouldn't budge. Emeralds would be considered dull and worthless when compared to that deep, stunning green. He couldn't speak. He couldn't swallow. He was lucky to breathe, which meant he was staring at her like a fool as she gave a little shoulder shrug.

"Spence, I'm not going to let you drive on unplowed roads the state patrol is about ready to close down anyway. I'll be fine here. Look, there's a vacancy sign. It's a nice place."

He tore his gaze from hers and stared at the stately hotel sign. Any second now the effects of Lucy would wear off and he would be able to speak again like a normal man. "What if the power goes off?"

"They probably have a generator."

"What about dinner? Have you had dinner?"

"Uh, no. There's a restaurant next door, oh, that's closed. No surprise there. Don't worry. I'm sure there's room service in a place like this." Kindly, she laid her gloved fingertips on his forearm. "Thanks for your concern, but I'll be fine. You can leave with a clear conscience. Really."

"Maybe I don't want a clear conscience." Even through the layers of down of his sleeve, he could feel the weight of her fingertips, the impact of her touch. It was like a mortar blast against the shields of his heart.

Wasn't that just his luck? She was the only woman who had ever made a dent in his defenses. A smart man would trust a grown woman to take care of herself, drop her off and drive away. But he'd never been a smart man. Doing the right thing wasn't always smart. He didn't like the idea of Lucy being alone in a hotel room when a blizzard hit the city. Sometimes electricity and services were running by the next day. Sometimes it took much longer. She didn't even have a change of clothes with her.

"Wait." He reached to turn on the radio and scanned for a road report. He found one of the local stations and listened. They were in the middle of listing all the county road closures. He thought of his brother-in-law, Jack, who would probably be called out on patrol tonight. The storm had come in fast, to everyone's surprise.

He could feel Lucy's gaze on him. His palms broke out in a sweat. There was that panic again, settling in because she was too close. Only the console separated them, but it wasn't only physical distance. He'd stopped barking at her and started caring, and he wasn't even sure when he'd allowed that to happen.

Maybe it was inevitable. He'd been watching Lucy from afar for a long, long time.

"I have three options," he told her, down to business and determined to stay there. That way he didn't have to notice how honest her eyes were. "One, we call my brother-in-law with the state patrol."

"Katherine's husband, Jack?"

"Yep. If he's not out on an emergency, he can probably take you home."

"I'd hate to trouble him. Someone might need him more than I do."

Sincerity. It made her seem flawless and even more beautiful. He swallowed hard, wiped his palms on his knees and stared at the hotel's sign again. "Option two: we take you over to stay with Rebecca. She's in a two-bedroom condo with a spare guest room. She's not far from here, and I'm sure she'll be glad to have you."

"Then I'm inconveniencing her."

"Lucy, you'll be inconveniencing me worse if you stay here. Hotels are fine, but tomorrow is Thanksgiving. What about your family? Here's your third option: I take you home. I've got four-wheel drive, and I'm not scared of a little snow."

"So I see. Actually, I'm surprised snow doesn't melt at your command."

"Actually, me too."

"Spence, I can't believe this. You're actually almost smiling."

"I've been known to smile."

"Not that I've ever seen. Sure, in theory of course you are capable of smiling, but not even I could imagine it." Were they having a moment together, Lucy wondered. Were they really getting along? "I'm guessing that you even have dimples."

"Shh, don't go around saying things like that. A man like me can't have dimples. That will ruin my reputation."

"Oh, so that's the secret to Spence McKaslin. The growling personality is all for the sake of your reputation." Lucy rolled her eyes. Men. "Don't worry. Your secret is safe with me."

"Thanks. I appreciate that. Word like that gets out and I'll lose all respect."

"I don't think you have to worry about that." Lucy felt a little flip-flop of her heart, and that surprised her.

Okay, maybe it was because she'd never seen this side of Spence before, but what she *did* know about him certainly made him a man to admire. He was devout and devoted to his family. He was active in his church and did extensive volunteer work. That meant he *couldn't* be a bad guy, right?

He hauled his cell phone from his coat pocket and punched a number. "I'll check with Rebecca first. Do you have family here in town that can pick you up tomorrow?"

Now was the moment of truth. "I don't have family in town."

"Oh, they're flying in?"

It was an assumption she should correct, but when she opened her mouth, she hesitated. Saying the words "No I'll be alone for the holiday" was hard. She had to gather up her gumption and just as she was opening her mouth to correct his misimpression, Rebecca must have answered her phone, because Spence started talking. Lucy could personally come up with a thousand excuses why Rebecca—she knew her from church and the bookstore, of course—wouldn't want to have her privacy invaded, but Spence snapped off the phone.

"It's settled." He didn't look at her as he put the truck in gear. "Rebecca is more than happy to have you. She got so excited I couldn't get a word in edgewise. If you have no objections, I'll take you there."

She thought of how difficult and dangerous the county roads were and then of Spence fighting them back to town. She looked up at the hotel, very nice but so impersonal—so lonely. "My cat will miss me, but I always leave plenty of food out for her. If I don't, she gets huffy."

Spence frowned, staring intently at the hotel sign.

"I'll take that as a yes. Do you mind if I stop by the grocery store? I was going to grab a bite to eat on the way home, but most places are closed."

"Sure, let's stop. That way I can pick up a few things, too." Shopping with Spence. How could that be fun? She tried to picture him doing something as ordinary as pushing a grocery cart—and she could as long as she imagined a frown on his face.

The traffic report droned on, filling the silence between them. Spence was absorbed in negotiating the slick streets. Snow fell harder with each passing minute so that by the time they climbed out of the truck three blocks away, she sank into snow up to her knees. And to think it had been sunny with blue skies only this morning.

She crunched in beside Spence, who stopped to make sure she didn't fall on the shoveled walkway in front of the automatic doors. The rock salt was having a hard time keeping up with the gathering ice. Once inside, Spence separated a cart from the others with a snap of his wrist and, with a commanding walk, took off in the direction of the bakery.

"Due to bacterial formation, you should always buy from the meat department last," he told her.

Yes, this was pretty much as she imagined it. She wasn't surprised when he hauled a list out of his pocket and, with a glance, headed off for the bread aisle.

She, being much less serious, lingered by the boxes of donuts. They didn't have the powdered sugar kind, so she chose a package of blueberry muffins with powdered sugar tops.

"Give them to me." He held out his hand.

"Don't tell me how bad these are for me," she warned him with a smile as she clutched her muffins.

"They aren't steel cut oatmeal, that's for sure." He took the package and set it in one corner of his cart, far away from his whole grain, extremely healthy kind of bread. "The next aisle over is coffee and tea."

"Oh, and hot chocolate." She led the way. The moment she turned the corner, she spotted Marin Baylor, youth pastor from the church, debating over two boxes of tea.

"Lucy." She looked up with a welcoming smile. That smile slid from her face like snow off a tin roof when she gazed over Lucy's shoulder. "Spence?"

Marin sounded a little shocked to see them in the same store together. It was the together part that was so shocking, apparently. "My car got plowed under. Spence is rescuing me."

"That's mighty Christian of him." Marin nodded thoughtfully. "Spence, did you get my message about Project Santa? I'm sure I'm on your callback list, but since we're face-to-face—"

"Yes, I meant to call you. The week got away from me." Now that he was speaking with Marin, the tension eased from Spence's jaw and broad shoulders.

He really is a handsome man, Lucy thought as she watched him reach into his other pocket and pull out a small notebook. He thumbed through it, pulled a pen out and made a note or two. It was church business, and she didn't want to interrupt or listen in, so she let her mind wander.

When exactly had he started avoiding her? She studied the man who looked so good in his black winter coat, trousers and black boots. He was in good shape; he probably was one of those admirable individuals who worked out and ate wisely all the time.

But what was attractive to her about Spence wasn't

his physical appearance. It was how he stood soldier-straight and full of honor. It was the respectful way he talked to women. It was the kindness he showed to small children. She'd seen him with his niece and nephew when they were in the store or at church. Why was a great man like him still not married? Aside from the distant and difficult personality.

"Well," Marin said. "I've got to get going. They're forecasting another six to eight inches before midnight. You two drive safe. See you on Sunday."

Lucy had time to say goodbye and give Marin a wave before the pastor was off, hauling out her cell phone. Spence, judging by the scowl building on his face, had noticed, too. Lucy feared the ramifications. "Do you think she'll tell Katherine?"

Spence shook his head. "This spells trouble for me, but I'm used to trouble. It's hard not to be with so many sisters. You must have siblings, too."

"One sister, but she and I are worlds apart."

"Some days I think I'm on earth and my sisters are on Pluto, but I don't think that's what you mean."

Who knew Spence McKaslin could quip? Lucy started down the aisle, wondering what other surprises might come her way. Spence always seemed so, well, grim. Maybe he was an interesting and potentially funny guy. "I'm the only Christian in my family. It annoys my mother to no end, who treats me as if I've been sucked into oblivion by a giant sea squid."

"Is that a roundabout way of saying she does her best not to talk to you?"

"Yep. My dad pretty much follows her lead. He's a pharmacist and somehow uses that as his reason why there can't be a God. Anyway, I'm not exactly banned, but if I announce that I'm coming home, there's this long silence and a polite, well, how nice. I'm sure we can make room for you." And exactly why was she telling him this? She didn't tell anyone this. Embarrassed when he didn't say anything, she turned the corner and headed down the milk and eggs aisle. She grabbed a carton.

He came up beside her and took one, too. "What about Thanksgiving? They're not flying in?"

"No." Now he probably thought she was someone who allowed deception. Her chest bunched up, making it hard to breathe. "I don't like to actually explain this to people."

"You mean to someone you don't especially like?"

"To someone I don't especially know," she said and wondered at the wince on his face—not a scowl. Spence might not be as grim and as emotionless as she'd always thought. "It's painful, and so I just try not to have to talk about it. You have a wonderful family. Your sisters adore you. You have the perfect parents. You are very blessed, Spence."

He shook his head. "Maybe you don't know that Dorrie isn't my real mother."

"No." She didn't know the family well, only Katherine. "I guess I just assumed."

"Nothing can hurt like family," he said quietly.

For a nanosecond, she heard something else in his voice and then in his silence, but he broke away and headed toward the packaged shredded cheeses. She went to grab a box of butter quarters, and the span of distance was between them again—not just a physical one but one far more significant.

It was hard to see much of anything through the amazing downpour of thick, continuous, wind-driven snow, but the condominium complex looked new and snazzy. Shrouded trees and bushes lined plentiful side-walks and walkways. Long stretches of white hinted at lush spacious lawns hidden beneath.

A front light flashed on, illuminating a snow-covered walkway and porch. Lucy unlatched her seat belt. This was it, where she and Spence parted company. At least the uncomfortable silence would be over, but that didn't make her feel any happier.

"I'll walk you in." Spence pulled the e-brake and turned off the ignition. Without the engine noise, the howl of wind and the ping of snowflakes sounded loud in the silence. He cleared his throat, looking pained that she was still in his company. "I picked up a few things for Rebecca at the store."

That was surprising. He said it casually, as if he did favors every day. Spence McKaslin was definitely a surprise. She grabbed her bag by the straps and heaved it off the floor. "Did you go shopping for anyone else?"

"Katherine needed a few things. I'll drop her stuff by on my way home. I don't live too far from her."

She had never given much thought to where Spence lived—in a cave, a townhouse, a tidy home in a cul-de-sac? She couldn't picture him anywhere. Spence McKaslin was more than a surprise, he was a genuine mystery and the opposite of what she expected. "If you live near Katherine, does that mean down the street? In the same subdivision?"

"Three streets down, five blocks over."

A homeowner, then. She still couldn't picture it. She was glad he hadn't insisted on taking her all the way home. The fifteen miles out of town and then all the way back across town would have taxed her conversational skills. Spence was not an easy man to chat with.

"Thanks for this. You could have left me to freeze beside my car."

"Sure, but then I would have had to deal with all my sisters. They would have been very mad at me." He almost smiled again.

Yep, there was a hint of dimples, just as she'd imagined. Their gazes met, and it was like a spark from a live wire against her soul. What she saw in that brief moment was Spence's heart—good and noble and lonely.

Lonely was something she knew a lot about.

"There's Rebecca." Spence gave a nod in the direction of the condo and yanked open his door.

Bitter cold and bulleting snow filled the passenger compartment. Through the haze of snow coating the glass, she could see Spence's hulking shadow cut around the front of the truck. She reached for the door handle, but then the door was already opening. Spence stood with his hand out, gloves on, to help her down.

"Careful, it's slick." That's all he said and tersely, as if she were annoying him.

She remembered the glimpse she'd seen of him. The hint of a smile, the niceness. She didn't take his gruff tone seriously as she placed her hand in his and launched off the truck's high seat. She landed knee-deep in snow, nearly blown over by the gusting wind, but Spence steadied her. He was solid and reliable, refusing to let her fall.

A haze of the porch light winked like a lighthouse's beacon on a far shore. Spence yanked his hand from hers and turned his back to gather the groceries from the backseat. He took hers, too, and walked alongside her so as to block the worst of the storm.

"Quick! Before you two freeze." Rebecca held the door open more widely.

Since she was already about to become a snow woman in two more seconds, Lucy gladly tumbled through the doorway and into the warm condo. Spence was on her heels, groceries in the crook of his arm. The door slammed shut. The arctic blast of the wind died. The last of the snow tumbled to the entry rug, and Lucy breathed a sigh of relief. A hot current of air blew at her ankles. Blessed warmth.

"Lucy, this is going to be so much fun." Rebecca took one of the grocery sacks from her brother. "I've got the fire going in the living room. The guest bed is made up with the electric blanket on high. I've got a pot of lemon tea steeping to warm you up. Spence, come this way and put that heavy sack on the kitchen counter."

Spence glowered. "I've got to hit the road. More stops to make before I get home."

Lucy struggled with her zipper, watching him through her lashes. The way he said it, no one would guess that he had groceries to deliver and family to check on. Or that he did so gladly. "Thanks again, Spence. You are my lifesaver."

"Next time pay better attention to the weather reports." He marched past her dripping snow on the carpet and disappeared into another room.

He said it as if she had majorly inconvenienced him. But she had this suspicion that wasn't the truth at all. What was Spence's truth? she wondered as she shucked off her coat and let Rebecca hook it over the back of a nearby chair. Spence was definitely a man of mystery.

He marched straight out of the shadows as if he were a part of it. He nodded to her once as he passed straight to the door. "Rebecca, let me know if you need anything else. I bought an extra flashlight and a pack of batteries, just in case."

"Oh, I didn't think about the lights going out."

He nodded as if he wasn't surprised by that comment and grabbed the door. The spill of overhead light shone on him just right—or maybe it was her imagination—but for one brief moment his harshness lifted, his gaze found hers and there was that vulnerable heart of his. It was simple to see his loving concern for his baby sister and his protective nature, and more.

Yes, she saw much more. Like a flash of concern for her, too. He was glad that she was safe from the hazards of the storm.

"Good night, Lucy," he said quietly, not harshly at all. He opened the door, the storm claimed him and he was out of her sight.

But not out of her thoughts.

Chapter Three

Between the heat from the fireplace and the comfort of the electric throw she was wrapped up in, Lucy was blissful. Add to that the pair of comfy sweats and warm fuzzy socks Rebecca had lent her, and she never wanted to move.

"That was Katherine on the phone." Rebecca swept into the living room with a tray of drinks and two plates of goodies from the grocery sacks. "She said Marin called her a while ago and said she had an interesting experience in the grocery store. I'm sorry, but she knows about you and Spence now."

"You say that as if there is something more at work than his stalwart Christian duty."

"There could be. Katherine couldn't remember the last time Spence gave a woman who wasn't family a ride, let alone went grocery shopping with one. He tends to keep his distance."

"*Tends* to keep his distance? Now that's an understatement if I've ever heard one."

"He's a pro at it. If it was an event at the Olympics, he would be a gold medal winner. For the last decade.

Maybe longer." Rebecca curled up on the opposite couch and stole a chocolate-covered marshmallow cookie from the tray. "It's just his personality. He's been that way as long as I can remember. He's the nicest guy beneath all the frowning."

"I'm beginning to notice that." Since she had a terrible weakness for those cookies, she had to take one and ignore the fact that she was supposed to be counting calories. "I get the feeling he doesn't want anyone to know the real Spence McKaslin."

"So, does this mean you like him?"

"Me?" Should the fact that she dropped the cookie mean anything? She hoped not. She snatched it up, hoping that her fingers were shaking because they had been so cold only a little bit ago—and for no other reason. "Please don't read too much into this. Spence told me the only reason he was helping me was because he didn't want all his sisters angry at him if he left me there to freeze into an icicle."

"Uh-huh." Rebecca looked like she didn't believe it not even a tiny bit.

Maybe it was the perfect time to change the subject. "How is Katherine doing? I haven't had a chance to talk to her this week."

"Well, don't you think it's time we fixed that? Come to Thanksgiving dinner tomorrow, and you can see for yourself."

Was that a twinkle of mischief in Rebecca's eyes or just a trick of the light? Lucy wasn't sure, but she did know one thing. "I can't go barging in on a family holiday. No way."

"Well, Spence told Katherine who told me that you don't have any family in the area."

"Did he? So this is his idea?" Her heart gave a lurch. She had no clue if that was a good sign or a very bad one.

"Oh, no. This invitation comes from Katherine. We're having dinner at her house this year. Besides, our family has grown so huge with everyone getting married that you won't be barging in at all. We'll hardly notice you in the crowd. C'mon, say yes. Please?" She polished off the last of the cookie in one big bite.

Lucy did the same. Maybe it was all that yummy chocolate and processed sugar, but she felt warm and wonderful and optimistic. What could go wrong? She could have a little turkey, have a chance to talk with some of her favorite people—Katherine and Danielle. With any luck, Ava would bring dessert—she owned the best bakery in town. It was all win-win and had nothing at all—nothing whatsoever—to do with the fact that Spence would be there, too. She didn't want to see the man of mystery again. Really.

"Sure," she said, reaching for another cookie. Yes, she was feeling exceptionally optimistic. "Why not?"

"Great. Everyone will be thrilled you're coming." Rebecca spoke around a bite of cookie. "Even Spence."

Even Spence. Lucy felt her heart give a little flip-flop again. She tried to tell herself it was only because she was curious about the man. Only curious. But she wasn't quite convinced that was the whole truth—at least not anymore.

The moment he caught the delighted grin on Katherine's face, Spence knew he was in trouble. "Was it Marin or Rebecca?" he demanded over the top of the grocery bag.

"Both, actually." Katherine's beautiful glow wasn't only because she was eight months pregnant but because she thought her great plan might actually be possible. "Remember last year when Lucy first joined my reader's group, I tried to fix the two of you up?"

"How could I forget?" Lucy was the last woman he wanted to talk about. "Don't get carried away. She needed a ride. I gave her one. She needed a place to stay. I found her one."

"Awfully Prince Charming of you to come to her rescue." Katherine pointed the remote at the television and clicked it off. "I'm sorry. I don't mean to tease you. I'm just so happy. Good things happen to good people, and you're a good man, Spence. You deserve someone nice."

He winced. He didn't know if Lucy was nice enough. He suspected he didn't even want to know the answer to that. He did know that he had to find everything wrong with her, every flaw, every fault so he could keep his shields ready, active and in place. Spending time with her had proved to him how necessary that was. "Do you know what I deserve? A quiet night to myself without all these errands I have to do for other people. For once I would like to be able to leave work and not have to rescue someone who got her car plowed under along the street and can't get home."

"Oh, no. Lucy did that? Well, she's from Oregon. It rains most of the winter there. She probably doesn't know."

"Now she does." He glowered, hoping he conveyed that he thought Lucy Chapin was nothing but trouble, which she was. Absolutely. "Is Hayden upstairs?"

"Studying for a chemistry test."

"I brought her some of that tea she likes and those chips. Good study food." He strode off to the kitchen, leaving his sister before she could get more information out of him. He was sorry she was put on bed rest, as ordered by her doctor, but there *was* a bright side to it. At least she couldn't come trailing after him demanding to talk more about Lucy.

Lucy. Just thinking of her made confusing emotions tangle up in his chest. She was like looking at an impossible crossword puzzle. She was like looking folly in the face. No, it was worse than that, he decided as he set the bags on the kitchen counter and started putting stuff away.

If she got close enough, Lucy could strip away his tough demeanor and matching scowl, which gave him comfort and a sense of safety. He remembered how she'd made his defenses buckle. How she seemed to see too much of him when they were talking. How his eyes involuntarily followed her whenever she was near.

Not to mention the panic. Lucy Chapin was his worst nightmare. If he let himself, he would really like her. If he let himself feel those emotions knotted up in his chest, he might discover that he could more than like her.

Danger. That's why his heart was beating like a war drum against his chest. That's why his palms were damp and his brain was a little scrambled. He wasn't about to let anyone get that close—not on his life.

He emptied the rest of the perishables into the refrigerator and folded up the bags. He knew Katherine was waiting for him because the television was still off. Since he had to walk through the front of the house to get to his truck, he had to face her. His motto had always been that a good defense was a stunning offense. Distraction, that was the key.

"Hey, Katherine," he said, even before he could see her. "Have you heard from Jack?"

"Not since he went out. He said he might be late.

There was a bad wreck on the highway with a tractor trailer rig, so that might tie him up until late."

"I'm worried about you." Which was the truth, absolutely the truth. "I know Hayden's here, but what if the lights go out?"

"I've got a flashlight on my end table and a book to read when my movie is done." She seemed wise to his ways and bursting with another question.

He had to keep talking and fast. One thing a man learned with so many sisters was how to head them off. "I'll be just a call away. The roads will still be a mess tomorrow, so I'll go out to pick up Gran early. We'll probably be here around ten."

"Sure, all of that is fine, Spence." Katherine's eyes were laughing at him. "You sure are trying hard to keep me from asking you about Lucy again. If it's too hard for you, I won't. I promise. I won't say another word."

"Thank you." Relief left him dizzy. "I just helped her out. I know you're happily married to Jack. I'm glad for you. But you've got to understand. Marriage isn't for everyone."

"So you keep telling me." It was concern that marked her pretty face. She was just about the only one he let fuss over him, and he recognized the look.

He stared down at his snowy boots. He didn't want her to see how much this was costing him. Nothing could hurt like family, he'd told Lucy, but it was so much more than that. He'd lost the ability to trust. To believe in another person. To really believe enough to stake everything on someone else. He was grateful his sisters had found good men they could trust, even love.

But he didn't believe in it. Love faded. Love ended. Love could tear a man's heart out. He'd seen it happen to his father. Spence zipped up his coat all the way and faced the door. He braced himself because he knew Katherine's question was still coming and it would hit him like a falling brick.

"You like Lucy, don't you?" Her question was soft with kindness and gentle with understanding, but that didn't stop it from being too personal.

Too touchy-feely. Too tied up in emotions. Life was better when you stayed in the concrete world. In black and white. Did he like Lucy? That was a question he couldn't answer. Because he would have to look at his tangled-up feelings. Because he would have to admit that his well-guarded heart wasn't defended enough.

How could he not like Lucy? She was pretty and kind and lovely. When she smiled, it was like the sun coming out on a cloudy day. Like snow on Christmas morning.

"I don't dislike her too much," he said instead, saying what he wanted to be true. What he had to make true. "You know I'm better off alone."

"I know you believe that, but—" Pity for him filled her eyes.

Pity. He hated it. "Don't look at me like that."

"I want good things for you, Spence. You work so hard for all of us. You are such a good man."

"If you go on about how I deserve good things, I'm not going to grocery shop for you again." It was an empty threat, and they both knew it.

She smiled. "Love isn't a bad thing, Spence. Look how it has changed my life. I'm happier than I ever imagined being with Jack as my husband and Hayden as my daughter. And this baby on the way." She rubbed her round stomach, lovingly. "You don't want to be alone forever, do you? Don't you want to be a father?"

"No." To be a father would mean he would need a wife, and he'd vowed never to marry. Who could he ever trust that much? There probably wasn't a woman on the face of this earth that he could believe in. At least, he was pretty sure he would never find one.

"Fine." Katherine wasn't easily defeated. "Then let me tell you a little about Lucy. She didn't have a close family growing up. Her mother hardly talks to her since she became a Christian."

He knew that. He didn't want to think that they had something in common—moms who had let them down.

"She volunteers a lot at the children's wing of the local hospital. She's very devoted to her work there. She moved here because she came here on vacation and said she could still see the old Wild West."

Deep down he wanted to like that about Lucy, that she could see Montana's heritage and history and respected it. But on a safer level, he couldn't let himself admit to such a thing. "Probably because she writes those historical books, moving here makes her job easier. That's all."

"Even you don't believe that one. I know you, Spence. You push everyone away. You keep all of us at a distance." There was more than pity on Katherine's face now. There was love. "Maybe you could try letting someone in. I'm not saying it has to be Lucy, but if you did, I don't think it would be a mistake."

His throat ached. He thought back over the evening with Lucy in his truck. She had a companionable air to her. She was easy to talk with—even if he didn't talk much. She was gentle and kind and funny. He had said more to her than he'd said to any woman outside his family in a good decade. She'd made him almost smile. At least twice. Maybe more. She made the cold places in his heart ache to be less lonely.

She was definitely a woman he needed to stay away

from. He swallowed hard against the emotion bunched in his throat and lifted his hand in farewell. "See you tomorrow, Kath."

The moment he felt the driving snow beat against his face, he tried to tell himself that Katherine might mean well, but she was wrong. He didn't need anyone. He was happy with his life. He was glad to be alone.

The trouble was that loneliness was getting bigger and bigger, and tonight it felt enormous. The wind howled, chasing snow into drifts as he fought through the accumulation to his waiting truck. The lights behind him faded into darkness. By the time he'd tumbled into the cab and started the engine, he was colder than he'd ever been. He wanted to tell himself it was the weather, but it was more. It was the loneliness beating at him, the loneliness that hadn't felt so bad before tonight. Maybe it was because he'd been so numb to it.

That was Lucy's doing, too.

He started the truck, letting the defroster blast on high as he wiped down the windows again with another towel from beneath his seat. It was impossible not to remember Lucy watching him as if he'd sprouted another ear when he'd meticulously wiped down his side of the truck.

He supposed a woman like her wasn't used to being practical. Katherine's words stuck with him and hurt like a blade dug deep. *Maybe you could try letting someone in. I'm not saying it has to be Lucy, but if you did, I don't think it would be a mistake.*

He couldn't imagine a bigger one. Lucy was a writer, an author. In that way, she was just like his mother had been. She was someone seeking attention and fame and all the things that didn't matter in life.

So what if he liked her? Nothing could ever come

of it. He wasn't foolish enough to let anyone too close to him—and never a woman chasing after dreams. No, he was a man who believed in what was real, in what mattered and in what could be measured by hard work. He didn't approve of dreams.

Snow beat with impossible force against the windshield, and he started out in low gear, going slowly. He struggled to see the road at all.

The darkness seemed endless tonight, and he felt small and alone as he drove three streets down and five blocks over.

"Let me know if you need anything, okay?" Rebecca was saying from the hallway. "There are extra towels in the side cabinets and a new toothbrush in the top drawer on the left side of the sink."

"You are very well-equipped for visitors." Lucy couldn't help being impressed. "My guest room is full of cardboard boxes I haven't unpacked yet."

"The munchkins stay over now and then. My nephew and niece," she explained.

"It must be wonderful that you're so close to them."

"And that's the way it's going to stay." She stopped at the guest bathroom door and stepped inside to put a new tube of toothpaste on the counter. "I'm getting married in January, and one of the first things Chad said when we were talking about how we were going to fit all his stuff in this condo was that there had to be room for the munchkins to stay over."

"And soon there will be more nieces and nephews to dote on." Lucy thought of the McKaslin twins, Ava and Aubrey, who were now both expecting.

"Yes. Spence has said that we're going to be outnumbered soon." There was an electronic chime.

"Is that your handsome fiancé?"

"Sending me a text message." Rebecca's heart-shaped face brightened with unmistakable happiness from unmistakable love. "That means he's home safe."

"He wants you to call him. Go." Lucy remembered what it was like to be young and in love. "I can take it from here."

"Thanks, Lucy." Rebecca was already heading down the hall. "Just interrupt if you need something. Promise?"

"Promise." Lucy stepped into the guest room with twin beds against two walls and a large window framed with floral-printed curtains.

She smiled at the flannel pajamas on the foot of one bed—still in its wrapping. Rebecca was surely a thoughtful hostess. The McKaslins were a nice family. She was looking forward to tomorrow, even when it came to Spence. He was a serious mystery, and the glimpses she had seen of him had more than intrigued her. They had shown her a snapshot of sorrow she could not help being touched by.

Everyone had a story; everyone knew sorrow. She knew that, but when it came to Spence, oftentimes it was easy to believe the cold, invincible face he presented to the world. She went to close the door, and the lights blinked out. Darkness descended, blotting out every shadow. She froze, disoriented. She didn't know her way out of the room, and if she took a step with her luck she would bang right into the door.

Rebecca's voice floated down the hallway. She was still on the phone. "No, sweetheart, don't come over. Stay where you're warm. Lucy and I will be fine. I've got a flashlight and batteries right here, thanks to Spence."

Spence. Thanks to him there was a small light flashing to life at the end of the hall, chasing away the darkness. Whatever his flaws, he sure took good care of his family. Why hadn't he married? Why did a bachelor own a house in a family neighborhood? Why did he walk around like a disgruntled grinch on Christmas Eve? Like Scrooge counting his money?

It was a mystery, and there was nothing she liked more—other than a good romance, but that went without saying. She opened the door and made her way toward the light.

Chapter Four

"Oh, I can't wait to meet this Lucy I've heard so much about." Gran tossed him the merry look of hers that said she knew something he didn't.

It was probably because she had called Katherine or Danielle or Rebecca, any of whom would have been more than happy to inform their grandmother about Lucy Chapin. Disgruntled, he gripped the steering wheel tight and took his gaze briefly from the road to give Gran the Eye, adding extra squint and heavy frown.

"What? You don't like Lucy?" Gran's wide-eyed innocence was not too innocent.

Yep, they had all been definitely talking about Lucy. He scowled. It was best to keep quiet. Anything he said would be misinterpreted. He knew this from vast experience. He stared at the road, hoping Gran would get the hint and change the subject.

"Lucy is quite successful, isn't she?" Gran's voice gave a little smile, as if that was a good thing.

"Success is a matter of opinion," he said. Even as he said the words, they did not sound harsh enough to his own ears.

"Oh, I think a person can be successful in more ways than one." Gran was practically singing she sounded so happy.

He rolled his eyes. What had his sisters been saying?

"Your grandfather was a very successful business-man by any standards, and yet he never once lost sight of the other ways a man can be successful." Gran paused, as if she were waiting for him to ask what those ways could be.

"The only success is not disappointing your family or God." Maybe that would stop her. "I'm not interested in Lucy Chapin."

"Why not? She sounds as nice as could be."

"Nice? Nice is not what I'm looking for."

"You can't fool me, dear boy. You are transparent to me." Gran's words warbled with love and delight.

Thank heavens the ride was over. He pulled the truck into Katherine's shoveled driveway and cut the engine. "Conversation over, Gran. Now don't you move a mus-cle until I get over there to help you down. It's slick as can be out there, and I won't have you falling."

"Yes, dear."

Her amusement followed him out into the bitter cold. Her mood seemed to hover behind him like those storm clouds overhead. There was no doubt about it now; he was in for a hard time today. The women in his family were probably planning his and Lucy's wedding. His pulse stopped. His foot slipped. He grabbed the bum-per for support.

Marriage. Now that was one trap he wasn't going to be lured into.

He opened the passenger door and helped Gran down. Jack had been out early and shoveled and deiced, but Spence wasn't taking any chances. He kept a good hold on his grandmother until they were safely beneath the porch's wide roof. He raised his hand to knock, but the door was already swinging open.

Ava's smiling face seemed to burst with secret happiness. Was it too much to hope that she was still ecstatic about her pregnancy? Or was it something else—like Lucy—that she was smiling about now?

"Gran! Right on time." Ava kissed their grandmother's cheek and drew her into the warm house. "You're looking more gorgeous than ever."

"So are you, dear." Gran took Ava by the hands and admired her. "I never looked so lovely when I was pregnant. Oh, and Aubrey dear, you look beautiful, too."

Spence stopped listening because his ears filled with static. That could only mean one thing—Lucy was close by. He couldn't remember closing the door or taking off his coat. His optic nerve hardly registered the sights of his twin sisters tugging Gran into Katherine's living room or the family greeting him. His eyes malfunctioned, and the only face he could see was Lucy's. Her emerald eyes and the cute slope of her nose and her gentle smile were powerful enough to make his feet stop moving and his throat go dry. He could only pray no one would notice, especially his eagle-eyed sisters.

"So you're Lucy." Gran's voice rose above the others. "What a pleasure to meet you. Danielle gave me one of your books just last week. I started it yesterday, and I can't remember the last time I read something that made me laugh so hard."

Here it came, the long stream of self-importance he knew had to be there. He turned on his heel, forced his feet to start working again and stalked from the room. He could hear his mother's voice from long ago, still crystal clear after all these years. *If it wasn't for you, I*

*would be a star right now. I have the face for it, every-
one used to say so. Then I would be somebody. Someone important.*

He was halfway to the kitchen, but was he safe? No,
because Lucy's voice was following him like a cloud
of doom.

"That's so nice of you to say. A lot of people tell me
my books are funny, but they aren't supposed to be."

A wave of laughter followed him as he stormed into
the back half of the house. Dorrie and Lauren looked
up from their work at the counter.

"Hi, Spence." Lauren repositioned her knife and kept
chopping. "Happy Thanksgiving."

"Happy Thanksgiving to you, dear." Dorrie's eyes
were twinkling, always a bad sign. She was in such a
happy mood.

He didn't approve of happy moods. The sound of
Lucy's voice seemed to gravitate to his ears like space
dirt to the atmosphere, and while he couldn't make out
the words, he heard kindness and caring in her tone.
Gran was answering her. They were hitting it off. Great.
That meant everyone in the family was now in love
with Lucy.

"You look in a particularly good mood this morning."
Dorrie waltzed toward him, stopping to lay a reassuring
hand on Lauren's shoulder before she circled around the
counter. "And wearing the sweater I gave you for your
birthday. It looks handsome on you, just like I thought."

"It's black. It seemed appropriate for today."

Dorrie laughed; she always understood him even
when no one did. It had always been that way, even
when he'd been a hurting teenager and he'd done his
best to push her away. She hadn't been fooled then, and
she wasn't now. "It may be an occasion of mourning for

you, Spence, but we like having Lucy here. You ought to try smiling a little. Show off your dimples."

"I don't have dimples." It was best to deny it.

"Put your best foot forward. The girls told me everything."

"Of course they did." He recognized the look. Dorrie was ready to give him a hug, and physical closeness made him nervous. He stepped back. "I don't want to put my best foot forward, sorry."

Dorrie rolled her eyes, still not fooled. "If it makes any difference, I don't think it matters. God makes our plans, Spence, we don't. Don't you forget that."

It was his turn to roll his eyes. "God's plan for me right now involves making sure no one falls on the sidewalk out front. I'm going to put more deicer out there before Danielle, Jonas and the kids get here. Jonas might have trouble with his cane."

"All right." Dorrie went back to the stove where pots were boiling, and delicious scents were rising up with the steam. "You go work on the sidewalk if that's what you need to do, but you're still going to have to come back into this house sometime. You can't avoid her forever."

His hand was on the doorknob to the garage before he realized two things. Dorrie and Lauren were exchanging looks that made him fear the worst: They were going to make sure it was impossible for him to avoid Lucy Chapin. And, worst of all, he had left his coat in the other room. He would have to walk past Lucy to get to it.

Maybe Jack had an extra coat in the garage, he thought, and yanked open the door. "Dorrie, don't you sit me next to Lucy at the table. You hear?"

"Sure, I hear you." Dorrie sounded as if she were enjoying this way too much. "But I am your mother, young man, and you will sit where I tell you to, and you will mind the manners I raised you with."

He had a few things to say to that, but the truth was anything he might say would hurt Dorrie's feelings, and he wouldn't do that on his life. So he left her to her victory and her hopes and stalked out into the frigid garage. He was out of luck. There was no coat or anything he could use anywhere in the neatly organized shelving. Dorrie was right. He couldn't stay outside forever. He hit the garage opener, and who was standing there holding his coat?

Lucy. He gritted his teeth and prepared for his system to go haywire. His palms went damp. His face felt hot. He suddenly seemed far too tall and big and awkward.

Dainty, petite Lucy was sweet and unruffled. She obviously wasn't having a problem functioning. No, she looked calm and at ease, without so much as a nervous flicker. She was wrapped up warmly in her parka and fuzzy hat, scarf and mittens—in neon blue.

"Your sisters thought you might need this." She held out his warm coat like a peace offering.

He did not want a peace offering. He wanted his system to return to normal. He wanted the static to clear from his brain and the panic to leave his bloodstream. He forced his feet toward her and plucked the coat out of her grip. "They forced you to bring this out?"

"You know they did. They all used the pregnancy excuse, and your grandmother simply shouldn't be out in the ice."

"It is getting colder out." It was the closest thing he could say to thank you. He was grateful for her concern about his grandmother, but that was as far as he was willing to go. It was best to keep the status quo of him disliking her and her avoiding him. He punched his arms into the sleeves of his coat. "You can go now."

She squinted her pretty eyes at him and folded her arms over her chest. The contemplative look on her lovely face made his stomach drop.

Uh-oh. He was going to get some comment on that. As he spotted the bag of deicer and strode toward it—alarmingly close to her—he could hear her mind working. The best defense was a good offense, so he started talking before she could start in. "Go. Just because I helped you last night doesn't mean I want you hanging around today."

"Sure, I see that." She winced, and there was a shadow of hurt in her soft green eyes.

It stung his conscience, but he had to set boundaries. He had to drive her away and keep her there because of the strange weakening in the vicinity of his heart. Every instinct he had began to shout *danger!* Longing eased to life in his soul—a deep, quiet wish that he could not allow.

"I think I have your number, Spence McKaslin."

"I doubt it." He grabbed the scoop inside the deicer bag and filled it. There was no way she could know his secret. No possible way. He straightened, doing his level best to keep his focus on the concrete in front of his boots. With great effort, he was able to walk right on past her like a normal, not interested, unaffected man.

He was careful to keep his back to her, though, as he scattered the pellets across the driveway. Her boots pattered on the concrete behind him. He could feel her intake of breath. She was preparing to say whatever she had been thinking so hard about, and he wasn't going to stand for it. He had defenses to fortify and shields to keep in place.

"Go in, Lucy. Go away." Those words didn't come out nearly as harsh as he wanted, and he winced. How was he going to drive her away if he didn't sound mean and unfriendly? Where had his commanding voice gone? Where was his embittered grimace? He tried to summon them up, but they were as frozen as the wintry world around him.

"You can growl and bark all you want. I'm not going anywhere." Lucy padded on by him in her expensive designer boots. She was holding a smaller scoop, and she had the audacity to sprinkle pellets, too. "You can't scare me anymore."

"Why not?" He deepened his voice and scowled extra hard.

"Because I have figured you out, Spence McKaslin."

"Unlikely."

"Likely," she corrected with the sweetest grin. She faced him with her chin set and her pretty eyes laughing at him. "You always used to make my knees tremble, and I did all I could to avoid you, but no more. Growl all you want. I'm not afraid."

His jaw dropped. He knew he was staring at her like an idiot, and if any of his family happened to be looking out of the front window at this exact moment, they would draw a much different conclusion. He probably looked like a lovelorn fool gaping at Lucy as if she were the loveliest woman on earth.

She did happen to be the loveliest woman on earth, but he didn't want to be caught staring at her.

She sashayed on by, heading straight to the bag of deicer. "You don't have to look so shocked. I'm glad I can now step foot inside the bookstore and the church without having to plan how to avoid you first."

"Maybe I want you to avoid me." His mouth felt

strange in the corners, almost as if he were trying to grin. Impossible. He forced the corners of his mouth down into a severe frown and cast the last of the pellets along the corner of the driveway.

"It was nice of you to help me out yesterday." She stopped at his side.

Way too close. His throat seized up. His lungs forgot how to work. His feet iced to the concrete. "N-no problem. I would do the same for anyone lacking good sense."

"I know." She didn't seem particularly bothered by his insult, as if she knew he didn't mean it. "I understand completely. It was nothing personal."

"Good." Whew. He stormed past her and commanded his eyes not to stray in her direction. He'd had enough of this malfunctioning eyeball problem. It took all of his effort to focus on the ground in front of him, and yet his vision strayed to her. He couldn't help noticing the way she stood like sweetness itself, framed with the background of pristine snow and beheld by the white mantle of snow clouds that were gathering. Dressed in her bright blue coat, she was like a dream, too good to be real and impossible to believe in.

You don't believe in dreams, he reminded himself as he snatched Jack's snowblower from its place against the wall. He'd lived his life this way, from the moment Linda—his biological mother—took off. He learned how foolish dreams were. He learned how fickle love was. A smart man didn't let his heart go warm and soft over a woman. He gave the snowblower a shove and burst back out into the driveway.

Lucy was watching him with a puzzled look. "The driveway is clear of snow. Even that little skiff of ice is gone, now that the deicer is working."

He scowled. Scowling was one of his most effective defensive tools. "Certain neighbors have not cleared their sidewalks. They ought to be fined."

"It's a holiday. Perhaps they are out of town."

"Then they should have arranged for someone to do it for them." Why was he getting so irritated? He hardly cared if the sidewalks were shoveled or not. What he cared about was clearing them for Danielle's family when they arrived. It was Lucy who was agitating him. "Why aren't you in the house with the rest of the women?"

"Why aren't you in the living room watching football with the rest of the men?"

"I don't approve of sitting around when there's work to be done."

"It seems to me, Spence McKaslin, that you don't approve of most things." She was amused at him, he could tell by the twinkle in her eyes and the grin playing in the corners of her pretty mouth. "I know what your sisters are saying about us. I overheard them whispering in the kitchen."

"Oh, here we go." He gave the contraption a shot of gas as he hit the starter. The snowblower rumbled to life like a Harley running out of gas, and it was just loud enough to give him time to get his anger under control.

"Don't worry!" She waltzed closer, leaning so close that the silken strands of her hair tickled his jaw. "I'll try to get them to understand."

He swallowed hard, not knowing what to do. Denial was useless. He had a crush on Lucy. No amount of defensiveness was going to stop it.

"I have got everything under control." She shouted to be heard over the rumbling backfire of the blower. "Just before I came out here, I assured everyone that we are *not* together. If I ever decide to fall in love, it will be with a warm, friendly, emotionally open man."

He broke into laughter. "Did they believe you?"

"It's a possibility. No one argued with me."

"No, how could they? I'm not a warm, friendly, emotionally open kind of guy." He grinned. "Thanks for telling me. Now I can enjoy my Thanksgiving meal without all this worrying about what my sisters are going to pull next."

"You have always been safe from me, Spence. You know that, don't you?" She tossed the scoop, and it landed with a plop in the deicer bag. "I'm not on the hunt for a husband."

"I thought all unmarried women were."

"Then I'm the exception to the rule." She watched his shoulders visibly relax. Poor Spence. He believed that. He must have a poor opinion of women and marriage. "When I decide to hunt for a husband, I'll set my sights on a quality man."

"Are you suggesting I'm not?" He was grinning wide enough to show that hint of a dimple again.

She forgot to feel uncomfortable around him when he smiled like that. "I'm just saying that I'm not looking right now. But as far as quality goes, you're a good man, Spence. You shouldn't work so hard to hide it."

"You've got me all wrong, Lucy." His grin disappeared right along with his dimples, but a crinkle of amusement remained in the corners of his midnight-blue eyes. "I'm cold, unfriendly, emotionally closed and proud of it."

"Saying it won't make it true."

"Sure it will. You have to think positive." He tossed her a wink before he strolled off, pushing the whining snow blower.

Why was she laughing? She didn't actually *like* Spence, did she? She watched him power the machine down the sidewalk toward the deep accumulation of snow at the property line. Snow sprayed in a stream from the mouth of the blower and beat against the snow-covered shrubbery, obscuring Spence from her sight but not from her thoughts.

He was definitely a quality man. Spence hadn't just done the neighbor's sidewalk but had moved on down the block, clearing as he went.

There was nothing he could do to hide all his goodness. It was his personality that was the problem. She wrapped her arms around her middle, shivered and hurried back inside the warm house where she had friends waiting.

Chapter Five

"Do you want some peas, Lucy?"

She put her butter knife on the plate and recognized trouble twinkling in Mary Whitman's eyes. The older lady was hopeful. It was a look mirrored on the faces of all the people seated around the lovely dining-room table. Lucy nudged the handprint turkey crafted by ˋyler in his kindergarten class to make room for the bowl of rolls.

"Thanks, Mary." She took the bowl from the well-meaning grandmother. Clearly, the whole family thought she was Spence's only hope, and they weren't taking no for an answer.

She spooned baby peas swimming in butter sauce onto her crowded plate. She really had told the truth. If she ever found a man to love again, it had to be a guy whose heart was wide open, who could genuinely be in love with her. She wanted true love. She wrote about it. She believed in it. She intended to settle for nothing less.

"It's so nice to have you here, Lucy," Mary said. "Are you a good cook?"

Oh, she knew exactly where Mary was heading.

She was assessing wife skills. Lucy put the spoon back into the bowl. "Do you know what I'm good at in the kitchen? The microwave."

On her other side, Spence gave a disapproving huff. The family burst out in laughter.

"You are too funny, Lucy," Katherine said from the other side of the table. "I bet you are an accomplished cook."

"If I have any cooking abilities, I'm going to soundly deny them. I have no housewifey skills whatsoever— or any that I will admit to." She shoved the bowl in Spence's direction.

Was that amusement sparkling in his eyes? Her fingers brushed his as she released the bowl. He was a marvel. The scowl on his face looked genuine, but she knew it wasn't. For a moment their gazes met, sharing the private joke. He understood without words what she was trying to do.

"That's too bad." Spence dumped peas onto his crowded plate. "Lucy, there's no way I can date you now."

"It's a blessing we're not together, then." She watched the faces around the table. The sisters were sharing knowing looks. Dorrie shook her head, her eyes full of love for her son, as if she wasn't buying any of it.

Mary chuckled. "None of us are blind, dear. We can see what you cannot."

"Help." Lucy turned to the man at her side. "I don't know how to make this stop."

The corners of his frown threatened to turn into a grin. "Neither do I. Welcome to my life."

"Now I understand the scowl." She watched his sisters dissolve into laughter.

"We're just curious," Ava spoke up, cheerful as always. "We can't believe you're here. With Spence."

"You are a brave woman," Aubrey chimed in.

"Spence has never brought a young lady to meet the family before," Dorrie added.

High hopes. Lucy understood what that was like. She had been there before, wishing for a happy ending even when all signs pointed in the opposite direction. That was why she was alone and why she'd returned an engagement ring. She couldn't bear to dishearten the McKaslin family, but it had to be done. "Spence, they know that I came with Rebecca, right? Not technically with you."

"Technically doesn't matter to them. They are women." Spence grimaced, looking like an angered grizzly.

"What exactly does that mean?" Lucy set down her fork.

The whispers around the table silenced.

"Uh-oh," Katherine winced. At her side, Jack hung his head, shaking it from side to side. Their teenaged daughter rolled her eyes.

A pained look swept across Dorrie's face. Spence's father, John, sighed in disappointment. Brice and Ava shared a sad look. Aubrey and William gazed at one another with lost hopes. Lauren, Caleb, Rebecca and Chad seemed horribly pained.

"Spence, I told you not to say anything like that." Danielle's admonishment came gently, with love.

"I'm just saying the truth." Spence looked formidable.

Lucy saw the crinkle of humor in the corners of his blue eyes. She couldn't help coming to his rescue. "It's a free country. Even a man like Spence is entitled to his opinions."

"He doesn't mean it, Lucy." Dorrie's motherly affection bordered on desperation. "Spence is the sweetest man—"

"Dorrie." Spence scowled. "Don't spread lies about me."

"Why, I would never lie. I—" Dorrie seemed truly distressed. "He's not so bad, Lucy. Trust me. You stick around, and you'll see."

"I'm terribly sorry, Dorrie, but I don't think I want to stick around and see." Lucy's gentle tone layered her words with kindness and understanding.

"She doesn't like me, Dorrie." He said the words as if they didn't hurt a bit. "It's not going to happen."

"Oh." Dorrie dipped her chin as if she had taken a blow but her voice was still loving. "That's too bad. I won't give up hoping for you."

I wish you would. He kept the thought to himself. The last thing he wanted to do was to disappoint Dorrie more. Sadness had crept into her eyes, and he hated that. "You might want to think about what you're doing, trying to fix Lucy up with me. Some women might take that as an insult."

"True. Poor Lucy." Ava was the first to agree.

"Yes, poor me! Maybe you all have been going about marrying off your brother the wrong way." He liked the way humor made Lucy's voice musical. She winked at him, a private wink that only he could see, before she turned to face the rest of the family. "You need to find a better match for him. Maybe there's a single woman somewhere who is looking for a curmudgeon. Think hard. Maybe you know someone."

Laughter roared around the table. He felt a few chuckles break free.

"Look!" Rebecca pointed accusingly. "Spence is *laughing*."

It was just his luck that someone noticed. He had to deny it. He had his reputation to think of. "It was an accident."

"An accidental laugh?" Judging by the look on her lovely face, Lucy didn't believe him one bit.

She was a smart woman but not that he was going to admit it. He dug his fork into the mound of mashed potatoes. His best defenses were up, and they were going to stay that way.

"Oh, ho." Gran sounded delighted. "That's a sign."

"It's not a sign," he barked through his mashed potatoes.

"Lucy, you ought to come to church with us on Sunday." Dorrie's hopes had apparently bounced back. "I'll host the family dinner, and you will be the guest of honor. John, tell Spence to be on his best behavior."

"I didn't know he had a best behavior," John quipped.

While his family laughed at him, Spence took it in stride. He couldn't say that he didn't deserve it. They could rib him all they wanted; he wasn't going to buckle. Although he expected better from his dad. Dad ought to understand his serious reservations with a woman like Lucy.

"I'm afraid I can't make it, Dorrie." Lucy's apology sounded sincere enough, and he closed his ears to the sound of her voice. He didn't want to listen to her. He didn't want to know anything more about her.

She was probably the kind of woman who worked all Sunday through. He supposed it took a lot of ruthless ambition to get where Lucy had in her career. No way was he going to have anything to do with a woman like that, except she didn't look ruthless.

He loaded his fork with more potatoes. He could see her out of the corners of his eyes, sharing words with Gran. The room around him went fuzzy and out of focus. The conversations around the table turned to static. The only thing he could see clearly was Lucy, golden and bright, in her modest forest green dress and a plain cross on a gold chain, looking like everything good and right in the world, like everything he had ever wanted.

Looks could be deceiving. He hardened his heart because he had to. He could not give in to the temptation. He had to stop liking Lucy Chapin. He had to get a hold of himself, make his brain and his eyes function correctly. He had to stop this crush he had on her; it was like a blight to his heart.

He grabbed his knife and buttered his roll. He just had to get through this meal. Then he never had to interact with Lucy again. He could go back to avoiding her at the bookstore and at church and snarling at her whenever she got into his path.

It wasn't ideal; it wasn't what he wanted, but it was the best plan he could come up with. Judging by the way his sisters and Dorrie were watching Lucy, as if she were their last hope, he had to do something and fast.

"How did you like the meal, Lucy?"

"It was delicious, Dorrie." She set the stack of plates on the counter next to the sink, choosing to turn on the water and let it warm instead of facing Spence's mother directly. How on earth was she going to talk to this woman? Anything she had to say would disappoint poor, hopeful Dorrie. "It was the best Thanksgiving meal I've had in some time. You are an amazing cook."

"Hardly, but that's nice of you to say." She set a tray of dirty dishes on the counter. "I hope you felt at home with us today. Spence comes across very brusque."

"He certainly does." Lucy turned on the faucet.

"He's a wonderful man. I keep praying for a nice woman to come along and see him for who he truly is."

"Then I will pray for that, too."

Dorrie sighed. "I see that you mean it. You really don't care about him?"

"Not in the way you're hoping. I'm sorry." She kept her tone gentle as she lifted the stack of plates into the sink. "I will be happy to help you find the right woman for him. There's someone for everyone. God didn't make us to be alone."

"No, He didn't." Dorrie sidled close, opened the dishwasher and tried to take over doing the dishes. "Tell me why you are all alone?"

"Sometimes love doesn't work out." Lucy held her ground at the sink.

"I'm sorry, dear. I really should do the dishes."

"You cooked. The cook doesn't clean. I have very strict rules about this."

A crashing sound rang from the dining room. Ava's "oops!" brought a round of laughter. Lucy ran a plate under the water. It was perfect timing for a subject change. "You had better go check on that, don't you think?"

"I'm going to let you have your way, dear, because I like you." Dorrie had the sweetest smile, exactly the one a loving mother should have. "But I warn you. I'm coming back."

"I'm still not going to let you do the dishes." Lucy

slid the plate into the dishwasher rack. Merry conversations rang from the adjacent room. As she scraped another plate, she couldn't help wondering what Spence was up to. Was he watching football in the living room with the other men? Or had he retreated outside again? And why was the back of her neck buzzing? Because Spence was standing in the archway, watching her with his X-ray vision.

The plate slipped out of her hand and landed with a *sploosh*. It was a good thing the drain had backed up or she would owe Katherine a china plate. Trying to pretend her hand wasn't shaking at the possibility of that shattered plate and *not* because of Spence, she hit the garbage disposal switch and let the chugging sound fill the silence. With any luck, Spence would be gone when she turned it off.

He wasn't. He was directly behind her. She knew because her nape was tingling again. She slid the plate carefully between the tines on the dishwasher rack and faced him. Water dripped off the tips of her fingers, but both the hand towel and the roll of paper towels were behind him on the opposing counter. Great.

Spence appeared disgusted with her. He whipped the hand towel off the oven handle and jabbed it toward her. "Here. Use this."

"Thanks." She grabbed for it, careful to avoid making the slightest contact with him.

"The state patrol is reporting that Blackhawk Hill Road is open and plowed. You can go home." He was like one giant rock standing in the middle of Katherine's kitchen—not a blink, not a breath, not the tiniest trace of a movement.

"Inside I'm sure you are overjoyed."

"Inside I'm dancing a jig."

"I didn't think you approved of dancing." She knelt to wipe up the few droplets she'd left on the floor.

"I don't." A muscle ticked in his granite jaw—just once. Then he went back to being stone.

You don't like this guy, Lucy, she told herself. So why was she struggling not to laugh? She tossed the towel onto the counter. "Thanks for the news. I'll finish helping out and be on my way."

"How are you going to do that? Isn't your car buried?"

"Minor technicality." She went back to rinsing plates. "I'll get a shovel."

"What exactly are you going to do with a shovel?" He scowled.

"The obvious. I'm going to dig out my car so I can go home."

"Do you know what wind does to snow?" He braced his feet.

"No, but it doesn't matter. I'll have to deal with it anyway." She turned her back to him with firm intention, as if to end the discussion.

Didn't she have a shred of common sense? He couldn't understand why she was being this way. She sounded upset—maybe at him, maybe at the snow. More likely it was because of what he'd overheard—and they both knew it.

He strained to hear down the hallway and the calamity in the other room was continuing—the happy sounds of the women as they laughed and worked together. He had a few moments before they interrupted. He took a step closer to Lucy. "Who was the guy who didn't work out for you?"

"Someone I was going to marry." She said the words quietly.

He had to strain to hear her. He couldn't tell if it was sadness or something like regret that hung in the air between them. He wasn't surprised she had been engaged, only that she never married. She was beautiful and enchanting and sweet as sunrise.

Too bad he didn't believe in the fairy tale of marriage. Just because it worked out now and then for the best didn't mean that it did most of the time. Plus, he had learned the hard way that what looked happy on the outside could, in fact be miserable on the inside. His dad's first marriage had been that way, and Spence had gotten an eyeful—enough that he could taste bitterness on his tongue after all these years.

Someone—it sounded like Ava—whispered, "Shh! We'd better stay in here. Spence is in the kitchen with Lucy. Alone. This may be our only chance to marry him off."

Had Lucy heard that? Maybe not, with the running water, but he had. His chest caved in. Pain exploded. Darkness beat at him. Marry him off? That's what they all wanted for him: misery and heartache? They wanted him to have the same life his father had had? He put his hand to his face, hating that it shook just a bit. He steadied it. "Why didn't you get married?"

"It's complicated." She started moving again, grabbing one plate after another and running it beneath the faucet. She had tensed up, though, as if he had hit a sore spot.

His head was ready to explode. He couldn't take it anymore. His family was in there meddling and waiting for him to fall for Lucy—as if he were desperate. The pain was building like the inside of a volcano, hot dangerous lava bubbling upward with enough power to blow off a mountaintop. That's how much pain he was under. That's what the thought of commitment did to him. He choked, wrestling down the past.

He watched her, debating what to do, as she rinsed another plate under the faucet. He was not going to think about how lovely she was. He was not going to remember how kind she was to his family. He was not going to let his crush soften him. A smart man would do anything to end this right here and now. Maybe then the pain building within him would stop. He prayed to heaven it would.

Forgive me for this, Lord, for what I am about to do. He couldn't see any way around it. A quick clean break would be the best for everyone. The pain blinded him. He wanted it to stop, that was all. He never again wanted to hear the words that had changed his world: *Love is pretending, don't you know that, stupid boy? You say you love someone and they give you what you want. Love doesn't exist.*

He hated that, after all these years, he believed her. That was the only time his mother had ever been honest. Love didn't exist, and whatever he felt for Lucy had to stop here and now. He took a deep breath, dug deep past the need to be kind to her—she was obviously hurting—and went for the jugular.

"The man you didn't marry, what was wrong with him?" He bit out. "Didn't he have enough money to satisfy you?"

She gasped. The plate slipped from her hand and shattered in the sink. The reaction was not exactly what he had expected. She was supposed to get mad at him and say it was none of his business—which would mean yes. Or she could lob a few uncomplimentary adjectives at him and shout that she never wanted to talk to him again. Mission accomplished.

Instead, she stared down at the sink horrified. Her entire being vibrated with pain, but she didn't speak of it. She gave a single sob. "Oh, look what I've done. Katherine's beautiful china. She's never going to forgive me."

He squeezed his eyes shut, unable to stand the look on her honest face. She didn't deserve what he had done. He turned off his heart so he wouldn't feel agony and remorse slam into him like a speeding semi. The drip of blood into the sink killed him.

What was it about Lucy? he asked angrily as he spun around and grabbed a few paper towels off the roll. She was contrary to everything he knew. She was a law unto herself.

"I—I need to buy her another plate," she sputtered, holding her chin very still and blinking fast. The tears in her eyes were because he had put them there. The fixation on the plate was to cover whatever damage he had really caused.

What damage could Lucy have? He always figured she was one of those perfect types that nothing bad ever happened to. Otherwise, why could she be so sunny? Why could she write fairy tales about love and romance that always ended with a happy marriage? She didn't exactly have her feet planted on the ground.

He took her hand in his—it was small and soft compared to his—and took a look at the cut. The cut was not deep, not serious, and it didn't look like there were any shards in the wound. He wrapped the towels around her palm and applied gentle pressure. "I'm the one who owes Katherine a new plate."

"But I dropped it." She focused stubbornly on the sink, turning her face away from him just enough to let him know she couldn't stand that he was so close to her.

He kept a tight hold of her hand so she couldn't pull it away. "I shouldn't have said what I did. I apologize."

"All right." Her chin lifted a notch higher. "I'll take care of this, thank you."

She meant her hand. That was killing him, too. This tactic had worked with every other woman who had crossed paths with him, and they all had cooperated nicely with his plan.

But not Lucy. Never Lucy. He should have known. A sigh of resignation escaped him as he lifted the towels from her skin. Most of the bleeding had stopped. It wasn't very much, but he hated the thought of what he'd done. He hated that he really hurt her.

"I'll get a bandage," he choked out. "Don't move."

He tossed the towels into the kitchen garbage and looked in the cabinet next to the stove. The first aid supplies were neatly organized. He loved Katherine and her organization. He took a bandage out of the box and a tube of antibiotic ointment.

A few more steps brought him back to Lucy, standing as still as the china plate and looking like she was in as many pieces. He hated that. Maybe her breakup with her fiancé had been fairly recent.

"I'm sorry, Lucy." He spun the top off the tube and took her hand in his. It felt cold, when a moment ago her skin had been warmed silk. "I wish I could take back what I said."

"You already apologized."

"I know." He didn't know how to begin to explain it. He had always been unlovable. It wasn't because he'd had a bad mother. She wasn't to blame for who he was essentially. He tried to be a good man, a good Christian and a hard worker for his family. None of that was Lucy's fault. Judging by the heartbreak on her face, she had enough pain of her own. He squeezed a few drops of cream onto the cut. "This won't keep you from your work, will it?"

"Probably. I may have to sue."

He detected a slight curve in the corners of her mouth—and what was wrong with him that he was still looking there? She was one woman he was never going to kiss. Let's face it. Neither of them would ever want that. He tore at the wrapping and peeled the backing off the adhesive. "Call the bookstore if you need the name of our lawyer."

"I might." Those tears still hovered in her eyes.

Deep down as far as his soul went, he wanted to make those tears go away. "There. You don't want to get that wet. I'll finish the dishes."

"No, I'll just use my other hand." She glared at him stubbornly—or more accurately, she glared at his left shoulder because she apparently couldn't look him in the eye after what he had said.

He wouldn't be able to either. He had never caused such harm before and that he had done it in self-defense brought him no comfort and no peace. He stepped away, tossed the paper in the can and searched for the right thing to say. Nothing came to mind. So he walked away and hooked his coat off the back of one of the bar chairs at the end of the counter.

The munchkins were outside making angels in the snow. He had promised to play with them. As he opened the sliding glass door, he watched Lucy. She was still at the sink, rinsing with her left hand, her shoulders as straight and as tense as a board.

At least he had accomplished his mission. She was

never going to speak to him again. He stepped outside and let the cold wind blow through him. The guilt remained.

Chapter Six

The image of the big bear of a man playing with his little nephew and niece remained with her through the long drive home. John and Dorrie had taken pity on her and offered to take her out in their four-wheel drive, bless them, and as she sat safely in the backseat of their SUV, she did her best to keep Spence from her thoughts. But was she successful?

No. Not even a little bit. How could the man who had bitterly and hurtfully said what he did be the same one who tended to her cut with such care? Who held her hand with tenderness? Who had made snow angels and then a snowman family with little Tyler and Madison, amusing them while they clapped and laughed and helped?

"Lucy, it's a pity you're not interested in Spence." Dorrie turned in the front seat as they bumped down the compact snow on the rural county road. "I have to say, you were our very last hope."

"Surely not your very last hope."

"No, there isn't anyone else. Is there, John?"

"No," John confirmed as he kept his eyes on the road.

"I think our boy has scared off every other eligible lady in these parts."

"And it's a pity, too." Dorrie looked truly wounded, sad for the son she must love like her own flesh and blood. "He's such a fine man, responsible and strong of character. Why, you can always depend on him. He never lets one of us down."

Those were exactly some of the traits Lucy had found herself admiring about the difficult man. But she couldn't forget what he'd said to her. She closed her thoughts, trying to keep those hard words silenced so they couldn't hurt her. "He's a little embittered."

"A little?" Dorrie twisted around again, "Dear, he's flat out the most bitter man I know. It was his mother. He never got over her abandonment. He drives women away on purpose, and I think it's so he won't have to risk being abandoned like that again. Don't you think, John?"

"That's what I think," John replied and lifted one hand to gesture to the road ahead. "Is that where I turn, Lucy?"

"Y-yes." She had to lean forward to peer between the seats out the windshield. She didn't want to give John the wrong directions. Dorrie's words were spinning around in her head. *He drives women away on purpose.*

"I don't know what we are going to do with him." Dorrie held up her hands helplessly, as if there was nothing more to be done for her son. "No one will have him. He's going to wind up alone and unhappy, and he will have done that all by himself. He doesn't listen to me. John, you have to talk to him."

"I'll talk to him," John agreed, but he sounded grim. "For all the good it will do."

"We have to try." Dorrie reached across the console and laid her hand on her husband's arm. "He's our boy."

"Yes, he is."

It was love, as deep as the heavens and as wide as the sky—for one another and for their son who tried so hard to be unlovable. Anyone could see it. Lucy looked away, feeling as if she were intruding on a private moment. She wrote of happy endings every day and the tough journey toward them, because she didn't have one of her own. Because she had to believe in a world where true love prospered and dreams came true. But today she hadn't needed fiction to find what mattered most. It was right in front of her.

"What a lovely home you have." Dorrie's words cut into her thoughts. "All those windows. You must feel as if you're living right in the middle of the forest."

"Sometimes I do." It was what she had loved about the house from the very first. The floor to ceiling walls of windows that peered out at the forest and, on the other side of the house, the breathtaking Rocky Mountains. The SUV came to a stop. "Did you two want to come in for a moment?"

"As much as I would love to, we don't have time."

"Then maybe another day." Lucy understood. She knew that the McKaslins had Gran to check on before they headed home, which was on the opposite side of town. "I'll take you out to lunch when the snow is gone. How about that?"

"I would love it, Lucy." There was no one more genuine or loving than Dorrie. It was easy to like her and admire her. "I hope you can make it to Katherine's shower. We would all love to have you there."

"I wouldn't miss it for the world." She gathered her things. The wind felt especially cold as she stepped out into the wintry world. "Thanks for the ride home, and drive safely."

"We will." Dorrie smiled and John nodded.

Lucy closed the door and stepped back. She figured Spence would look like his father one day in the far future, still strong and impressive with a head full of salt-and-pepper hair and quiet dignity. She searched through her purse for her house key, looking up to see them bump down her driveway through the drifted snow and disappear around the cedar grove.

She was alone. She sighed, not at all sure what she was feeling. Residual upset, from her encounter with Spence. Contentment, from spending the holiday meal with the warm and fun McKaslins. Regret, because her life was turning out so different than she had hoped.

She breathed in the winter air scented with snow, evergreens and wood smoke and let it soothe her. Snowflakes, dainty and airy, drifted against her face like tiny touches from heaven. The forest around her seemed silent and waiting, and the sky felt watchful as if hope was just around the corner.

There was an angry thump on the window behind her. She didn't need to turn around to know it was her cat, undoubtedly peeved with her extended absence. Sure enough, a fuzzy gray face stared out at her. Dark eyes gave her a scolding look.

"Sorry, Bean." Lucy waded through the deep snow on her porch, unlocked the door and tumbled into the welcoming warmth.

Home. She dropped her things on the bench by the door. The cat hopped onto the bench with a loud thump and meowed sharply. The Persian gave her an appraising look.

"I know, I'm in the doghouse." Lucy shucked off her

coat and ran her fingers across Bean's silky head. The cat flicked her tail, scowled again and jumped down with a four-footed thud. She walked heavily across the carpet, making enough noise to show her discontent.

Funny cat. Apparently, Lucy's stay in the doghouse was going to be a long one. She dutifully followed the imperial cat through the living room, the view of snowy trees and winter white was like looking at a picture, and into the kitchen where the cat's dish was empty, except for the broken scraps of kibble the princess would not deign to eat.

"My apologies," Lucy offered. She didn't comment that there was still plenty to eat in the bottom of the bowl. She filled it and set it before her cat. With a flick of a tail, Bean inspected her kibble and stormed away, still perturbed, apparently. Her padded paws made enough noise to echo in the quiet house as she disappeared down the hall.

Fine. She was on her own for awhile. She wrapped her arms around herself. All around her were windows. Tiny flakes winged to earth like poetry, and she let the serenity of the landscape, of the meter of the snowfall and the sweeping grace of the mantled fir trees lull her. But as beautiful as it was, it wasn't enough to draw her away from the cold pit of pain dark and deep within her.

Spence had done that, stirred her up with his callous words. *The man you didn't marry, what was wrong with him?*

No, Spence hadn't meant to harm her, she realized; he had meant to drive her away with a harmless insult. He couldn't know what she had lost. The ache sharpened, the one in her soul she tried to silence, and most days she was fairly successful.

But today she heard that ache like wind through the

trees. She padded to her bedroom and pulled open the bottom chest drawer. In the back tucked away, with other remembrances of dear moments of her life, was the picture still in its frame.

She brushed her fingertips across the smooth glass. Time had forever frozen the image of a much younger her, when she kept her hair long and when love used to light her up like midsummer. Her soul ached seeing the little boy with tousled black hair and big chocolate eyes, just like the man also in the picture. Their dear faces, one strong with character and heart, the other, sweet with a child's innocence, made her vision blur.

There were some things prayer couldn't fix. The sharp ache of loss that followed grieving and acceptance was one. Time could not heal it, only dull it. Some losses stuck with you forever, and you were never whole again.

It was dark by the time he had dug out the apple-green car enough to get the driver's side door open. Snow had drifted against the car, so he'd had to shovel that away too and his frostbitten hands felt numb, thick and useless as he fought the door handle.

Lucy. He had done his best to avoid her the rest of the time at Katherine's. It hadn't been easy. His gaze had continued to malfunction, automatically finding her whenever she was in his visual field. The buzz that filled his brain when he spoke to her had become permanent. He could remember how delicate her hand had felt in his. If only he could forget.

He dropped into the driver's seat and yanked off his glove. His right hand was red from cold and numb enough that it took three tries to get the key Katherine had procured for him into the ignition. The engine turned over, the heater blasted on and an upbeat song blared through the speakers. He hit that off, turned the heater to Defrost and hit the headlights.

If he had been trying to get Lucy out of his head and out of his life, he had failed. Her car smelled like her—like lilacs and sunshine and sugar cookies. A tiny crystal angel hung from the rearview mirror, swinging on a length of apple-green yarn. A pile of paperbacks was strewn haphazardly over the front passenger's floor, and a pile of notes written on flowery note paper littered the front passenger seat. The top note said—not that he was snooping, but his eyes happened to notice—idea for next story: a bookstore? Or a coffee shop. Check out Ava's bakery for research.

That explained the sugar cookie smell. He noticed a small bakery box in the backseat—sugar cookies from Ava's shop.

He scowled and searched the dash for the rear-window defroster switch. It was self-defense that had him gathering up criticism at her car—further evidence why he should not be interested in sunny, gentle-hearted Lucy. She left her books on the floor. That was no place for a book! Look at the paper she wasted and tossed around and left in a heap, besides lacking the basic common sense not to park on the street when the snowplow would be coming by.

None of it worked—mostly because his heart wasn't in it. All he could see was the image of her standing at the sink, rinsing plates and bowls, glasses and silverware with her left hand, waving away every offer to take over. She had washed the hand washables, wiped down the counters and helped Dorrie fill bags of leftovers for everyone to take home. If he had dared to get close enough to her, he would have witnessed the lingering sadness in her jeweled eyes.

He couldn't forgive himself for that. He laid his forehead on the top round of the steering wheel, hating what he had done. He had grown hard-hearted. Lord help him, because he didn't know what to do about it.

"Spence?" A familiar voice called out. Boots crunched through the snow.

"Caleb." He was glad to see his brother-in-law. Caleb, a city cop, was suited up in his uniform and cold weather gear. Spence angled out of the little car and grabbed the ice scraper from the roof, where he'd left it. "Good to see you hard at work. Too bad you left before dessert."

"Dorrie promised she would send a few pieces of pie and chocolate cake home with Lauren." Caleb had a quiet, confident air about him. He made a good match for Lauren. "This isn't your car. Wait—it's Lucy's. She was talking about being plowed under."

Great. Spence grimaced and put a cold frown on his face. Best that Caleb didn't guess as to the real reason he was out here on a holiday in subzero temperatures scraping the packed ice and snow off of a woman's windshield. "Thought I would nip the problem in the bud."

"The problem? You mean Lucy is a problem?"

"You know she is. You saw what went on." Spence put some muscle into it, and all he could do was get the smallest chip in the inch-thick ice. "You didn't help matters at dinner. You could have spoken up and saved me from the marriage-crazed women at the table."

"Hey, I figured the least said the better." Caleb held up his gloved hands as a show of innocence.

"I could have used some support. We men have to stick together." He gave the ice another swipe of the scraper. Nothing. "Dorrie practically has me married off to her."

"Marriage isn't so bad, once you get used to the misery."

"Funny." He wasn't in the mood for humor. In fact, he was starting to be opposed to humor of any kind.

"In fact, you sort of become tolerant to it. It's not so bad after a while."

Was everyone in his family a comedian? He began beating at the ice with the scraper. Tiny flecks sprayed off. At least he was making some progress. "When do you get off your shift?"

"Late evening."

"Then you can make yourself useful." Spence did his best not to grin. He knew he could count on Caleb to help out, but for some reason it was easier for him to demand it instead of ask for it. "I need you to come out with me and drop off this poor excuse for a car so I have a ride back."

"Sure. This is an excuse to see her, isn't it?" Caleb placed his hands on his hips, looking authoritative, as if he had everything figured out.

Hardly. Spence growled as the ice began to crack away. Victory. "Lucy Chapin is a nightmare. She's not the kind of woman I would pick—*if* I ever decide to marry and be miserable like the rest of you."

"I don't know. A guy who looks the way you do can't be too picky. Seems to me Lucy is out of your league."

"Thank you. Of course she is. She's too good for me." Finally some common sense. "I've been waiting for everyone else to notice that, but they are blinded by the thought of another wedding. What is it with women and weddings?"

"No idea, but after having one of my own, it *was* nice."

"So close. For a minute there, I thought we were on the same page, Caleb."

"Marriage isn't so miserable."

"Sure it is." And if his dad was happy in his second marriage and if his brothers-in-law were always grinning, then he didn't have to put that into the equation. "I'll be at the bookstore. Swing by when your shift is done."

"Working late?"

"Tomorrow's a big shopping day. We open at seven."

Caleb trudged through the snow to his cruiser parked on the other side of the street. Spence shook his head, sweeping the last of the ice flecks from the glass. He must really have been lost in thought not to notice his brother-in-law drive up. It just showed how much this thing with Lucy bothered him.

He waded around the side of the car, working on windows and wrestling down thoughts of her. Of how lovely she looked when she laughed, how nice she was to his family, how everyone loved her.

You don't have that crush on her any longer. He took up the shovel and dug into the snow in front of the low-slung VW. Every strike of his shovel into the hardpacked snow was a reminder he was only fooling himself. He wouldn't be out here frozen to the bone and so cold he could no longer feel half of his face for any other reason.

Maybe he *was* sweet on her, but he wasn't going to let a woman like Lucy get anywhere close to him. He would not be lulled by the sadness he'd seen in her eyes or by the bite of his conscience.

Once he'd cleared a path in the snow, he tossed the shovel in the back of his truck and folded his big frame into her little front seat. He shut the door, and everything Lucy surrounded him—her sweetness, her sun-

shine, her memories. His chest tightened, but it wasn't
the feel of his heart longing.

No, it couldn't be. He had grown too hard for that. A
heart made of stone could not love. It was as simple as
that. He put her car in gear and guided it out onto the
street, closing down every thought of her. Every feeling.

It was the smart thing to do.

With her laptop on the coffee table plugged in to the
Internet and the TV blaring the dialogue of a romantic
comedy, she shoved the dessert plate away. That chocolate cream pie was heavenly, but her waistline was not
going to thank her tomorrow.

She took a sip of tea and frowned at the screen. She
had e-mail waiting from friends she had left behind in
Portland. She knew every one of them was going to ask
why she didn't come visit for Thanksgiving.

She thought of Jim and his son, and it was like jumping off the edge of the earth. It was easier to be here,
where there were no memories of happier times and
of sadder ones. It was why she was putting off reading her e-mail.

"Rrowr." Bean nosed in and stood awaiting attention.

"Oh, so now you're talking to me." Lucy obliged
by running her fingers through the soft long hair. "I'm
sorry I left you."

The cat slitted her eyes and hopped away to the window seat. The blinds were drawn, but a sudden ray of
light glanced between the slats. Strange. Nobody ven-
tured down her driveway, especially in this weather.
She would have dismissed it as the neighbor kid, whom
she paid to plow her driveway, but he had already come
and gone. She set her cup on the coffee table, uncurled
her legs and crossed the room.

She lifted a slat and peered through the blinds. It was dark out and a truck's headlights sliced through the inky blackness with eye-hurting brightness. A door slammed shut, drawing her attention toward the garage. She recognized the curved hump of her car, dark as the night, and a tall, broad-shouldered form hiking away from it.

Spence McKaslin. Her pulse skipped five beats. Shock drew all the air from her lungs. Rooted to the floor, she couldn't move as he swung up into the passenger seat. For a moment, the overhead dome light haloed him. She could see the cut of his high cheekbones, blade-straight nose and the snow dusting his dark hair.

He really was a handsome man with classic rugged good looks combined with a masculine strength of character that gave him a hero quality. Her soul sighed against her will. She thought of what Dorrie had said, how he pushed women away on purpose. She was deeply sad that his ploy had worked.

She should let go of the blind slat and step away from the window, but some unknown force held her in place. It wasn't curiosity. She couldn't put her finger on why, but she watched as the passenger door swung shut. The dome light illuminated him as he reached for his seat belt, turning toward the house and toward her.

Their gazes met. Her blood pressure fell, pooling in her toes. She saw the bleakness in his blue eyes and in his heart. The passenger light blinked out, and he was gone from her sight.

She stepped away from the window, and the blind slat remained, stuck in place like a peephole. The truck turned around and lumbered off, the taillights brilliant pinpricks of diminishing light. They grew smaller and smaller until the night swallowed them, and she was alone again.

Chapter Seven

"I need to talk to you."

Spence snapped his briefcase shut and scowled at his sister standing in his office doorway. Danielle had been especially perky all morning long. While he was glad she was happy, he wasn't sure he approved of happiness—or at least not when there was work to be done. The Christmas shopping season was in full swing, and they were busy.

"I have no time. You'll have to talk with me on the way to the church," he said and grabbed his winter coat. "If you need to hire more help, then handle it. I have a folder of applicants in my top left desk drawer."

"Excellent. I have been hounding you for the last two weeks, you know."

Yeah, he knew. He was tired of hearing it. She had worn him down. "We have a bottom line, don't you forget it."

"Impossible with you here to remind me, brother dear." She smiled sweetly. Wearing Christmas colors of red and green, she was positively glowing. He had never seen her look better.

"I'm glad to see you're happy again, Dani. It's been a long haul for you and Jonas."

"Our lives are almost back to normal. We'll hear on his job situation late next week sometime." Danielle was always going to be the eleven-year-old sister he remembered with light brown curls and a quiet smile, regardless of how the years passed. When Dad had married her mom, life had changed for the better in the McKaslin household. Of all his sisters, Danielle was the most sensible—not that he was sentimental or anything. To prove it, he scowled. She was blocking the doorway. "Just don't go walking off the job and leaving me high and dry without a manager, you hear?"

Her hand landed on his wrist, stopping him from trying to shoulder around her. "I would never do that to you, Spence. You know that."

He did. "Are you ready? You don't have your coat."

"I told you we need to talk before *you* go."

"*We're* going to be late to the meeting. The committee head has to attend. You have less than three weeks before Christmas."

"There's something I need to tell you." Danielle looked apologetic.

Uh-oh. "You're going to bail on the committee, aren't you?"

"I've already spoken to my second-in-command, and she is going to sit in for me this morning. She has all the notes."

"You can just stand there smiling like this is great news. Why are you bailing on me?"

"I need to take it easier these days." She gazed up at him expectantly, and there was quiet joy on her face.

"You're pregnant, aren't you?" He frowned harder. He loved being an uncle, so this was good news. But as the manager of the bookstore, he was losing yet another assistant manager to motherhood. "Who am I going to get to replace you? I've run out of sisters. Not that a one of you is useful, getting married and leaving me with a store to run and no one to help."

Tears sparkled in Danielle's eyes as she went up on tiptoe, understanding perfectly what he could not say. What he could never say. His chest felt battered by a hurricane, but he made sure he couldn't feel a single lick of emotion.

"I love you too, Spence." She kissed his cheek, squeezed his wrist and walked away.

Sisters. He swallowed hard and closed the door behind him. He didn't know what he was going to do without them. They were all married, becoming mothers; they didn't need him anymore. He was in an especially fierce mood as he headed around the front counter and across the floor, briefcase in hand.

He had nothing but more problems. Before it was employee staffing deficits, and now he had to find someone to fill in her place at the committee. With any luck, whoever was second-in-command could step up and fill Danielle's shoes. He certainly wouldn't do it. He was strictly managerial.

He pushed through the door and into the bitter wind. The snow had hung around, but the sun was beating down with blinding brightness. An apple-green Beetle crept through the parking lot. He froze, panicked. Lucy.

Mercifully the car kept on going. He got a glimpse of the driver as it passed by—a brunette. It wasn't Lucy. There was a MSU bumper sticker, so he knew it wasn't even her car. He was safe. Whew. His knees were watery as he walked to his truck and unlocked it. There was no sense trying to purge her from his thoughts. He had been trying since Thanksgiving, but it was impossible.

He climbed behind the wheel and started the engine. All he could think about and all he could see was Lucy standing at her window, peering at him between the blind slats. Her big, soulful green eyes had watched him with a look he could not name, but it was one his heart felt.

One his heart *still* felt. All his defenses were like ice cracking away. He didn't know why he hurt so much. Maybe it was from a lifetime of not letting himself feel a thing. Perhaps, too, it was something more. It was that he wished things could be different. He wished he could take back what he had said to her. He wished he could have held her hand a little longer.

It was a good thing none of his family knew that little tidbit. He wheeled out of the parking lot, turning his thoughts to Danielle—good for her. She and Jonas had wanted another child. Katherine was due in a few weeks. The twins were both due in the spring. Life was changing for the better. So why did he feel stuck in place? Left out?

It made no sense. He didn't want to get married— end of story. He could never trust a woman that much.

The minute he pulled into the Gray Stone Church's parking lot, Spence knew something was wrong. But what? He whipped into a parking space by the church's annex door and grabbed his briefcase. The feeling that something was wrong remained as he launched out of the truck and into the airy snowfall.

The minute his boots hit the powdery snow, he knew what it was. He was staring directly at the passenger door of an apple-green VW bug. He knew that car. He had driven that car. There were books all over the front passenger floor.

Lucy. His heart gave one final beat. Dread filled him like water in a barrel. His feet carried him over the curb and onto the sidewalk, but he wasn't aware of it. He was too busy thinking of all the reasons why she might be at the church on a Wednesday morning because there was no way she would be at the meeting—none at all. She had never been at a meeting before. Suddenly he was at the door without remembering how he got there.

Lucy. He could see her through the window in the door. Dressed in a sort of white fuzzy sweater and black jeans and fashionable black boots, she looked as if she could have stepped right off the page of an elegant magazine. Casually styled hair fell in artful curls around her heart-shaped face and her emerald eyes were warmer than any jewel, deeper than any he'd ever seen before.

Why exactly was he noticing? The toe of his right boot caught on the lip of the doorway. He stumbled into the room. Typical. Lucy scrambled his system as effectively as crossed wires. His ears were buzzing. His head was in a fog. What was a man to do about that? He had a meeting to attend. He had to pull himself together.

"Spence?"

Suddenly she was saying his name. Whoever she had been speaking with had gone into the conference room. They were alone in the hallway with his words from Thanksgiving afternoon echoing between them—with the memory of her hand in his and her unshed tears.

"This is going to be awkward." She didn't look at him.

He tried to concentrate, but it was impossible with all the static in his head and the sharp bite of his conscience. She really didn't like him now. He could see it on her face. Once, he would have cheered about it. Now he felt small. He didn't like it one bit. "What's going to be awkward?"

"Didn't Danielle tell you?" She looked down at the floor between them. She was little, for all her bubbling energy and life. She was slim and small-boned, and when she was quiet he saw a depth in her that drew him a step closer. That made him want to know her better.

"I'll probably be taking Dani's place as the chair."

"What?" The word came out like a thunder clap. He ground his teeth. That sister of his. She set him up. "I'm going to have to disown Danielle from the family."

"Something tells me that's just bluster. Danielle cares about you. Why? *That's* the real question." Her chin went up, and there was a challenge in her eyes but no malice in her words.

It was almost as if she were blustering, too. All right; he deserved that. He could be a good sport. "I've been asking that question for years. Dani won't stop liking me no matter what I do."

"She has your number, Spence McKaslin." She almost smiled. It hovered in the corners of her rosebud mouth and in the gentleness of her voice.

His eyes smarted. He knew in that moment she had forgiven him for what he had said. Gratitude gathered in his throat, and he didn't try to speak. She had a generous heart, and he was indebted to her for it. He was a hard man to forgive. No one outside of his family had ever managed it.

He wanted to thank her, but he didn't know how. It would probably make him look like a pansy if he did, so he held his ground and his frown, although he instinctively knew that didn't fool her either.

"Thank you for delivering my car. That was a lot of trouble for you to go to."

"It wasn't so much." He shifted his weight, looking uncomfortable. "I didn't want your car blocking the entrance to the parking lot."

"Sure, I understand." As her car had been nowhere near to blocking the entrance, she got what he was trying not to say. He had called a truce, and that worked for her. "The children's wing of the hospital is very important to me. I was behind the scenes in last year's Project Santa."

"I see. You've been helping Danielle?"

"Yes." At least she wouldn't have to have too much contact with him. He would probably be overseeing the budget and the project's progress and nothing more. She wasn't sure how she felt about that, but she would have to be an insensitive clod not to have seen the apology and remorse on Spence's face when he'd walked into the church hall. He also had to have done a powerful amount of snow shoveling to free her car. That, in her book, was the sign of sincerity. "I have all the information I was compiling for Danielle. Including the funds request."

"That's a relief. Thank you, Lucy."

"Let me assure you, we won't have to cross paths often. I have everything ready to go."

"Good." The tension eased from his shoulders. "This won't be the kind of crisis I was fearing."

"Do you always fear crisis?"

"Don't you?" He appeared dead serious, standing as tall and as immovable as a mountain.

"Not always. Sometimes it is God's way of pointing us in the right direction." She might not have any clue what her own personal direction was, but God was at the helm so she wasn't too worried. What she did worry about was if Spence was going to let her stay on the project. "You aren't going to ask me to step down, are you?"

"Never crossed my mind." He was pure sincerity.

This man was more and more a puzzle, one she could not afford to start liking again. This was a man who was hurting and had hurt her out of his own pain. She did not need that kind of man in her life. "Again, this project is important to me."

"How long have you volunteered?" he said that as if she had just announced she was a former citizen of Mars.

"For a long time. I believe in living a purposeful life and helping others."

"So do I." A small smile softened his granite face.

He really is a handsome man, she thought, unable to help herself. She didn't want to like Spence, but she did understand him. "I think they've started the meeting without us."

"Oh." He looked around, the movement scattering thick locks of his dark hair. He moved past her like a man of steel, in control. His voice sounded like iron. "Follow me."

The order boomed down the hallway, and she resisted the urge to give him a sound retort, but she bit her bottom lip to keep it in. The project was more important. If only she wasn't so confused and frustrated, she might be able to figure out the best way to handle this man. She wanted a truce with him. A part of her saw how he was hurting and understood it too well. She battled the same feelings once. Bleakness and sorrow had nearly taken all the good from her life.

She forced her feet down the hall and followed Spence into the conference room.

* * *

I believe in living a purposeful life and helping others. Lucy's words were tormenting him, rolling around in his head. Spence leaned back in the chair, unable to force his gaze from the woman across the conference table. Light spilled onto her blond hair like liquid gold, framing her heart-shaped face and big, caring eyes.

You do not like her, Spence. He was resolute. You cannot like her no matter what.

"Spence?" Pastor Mark was looking at him expectantly.

They all were. Spence scanned the familiar faces around the table and gulped. How had he let his mind wander away from business at hand? He was not that kind of man. He was not prone to mental wandering of any kind. He did not approve of daydreaming.

"Spence, is this all right with you?" The pastor was still waiting for an answer.

To what? He didn't have a clue. He looked around the big table, hoping to glean some sort of hint as to what he was agreeing to, but nothing. There were just expectant faces smiling at him, pleased with something. He wasn't about to admit he hadn't been paying attention. He didn't approve of people who didn't pay attention.

"Ah, sure," he finally said, annoyed at himself. He wasn't about to let anyone else know he'd drifted off. "It's fine."

"Wonderful. That's just what I've been hoping for." Pastor Mark smiled warmly, and the rest of the table nodded and murmured in approval. "You're an excellent leader, Spence, and no one can manage better than you. But I think a hands-on approach, pushing up your sleeves and working with the people we are helping is just what you and the program need."

What? He blinked. Hands-on approach? Pushing up his sleeves? Working with people? What had he agreed to? At the edge of his vision, Lucy pressed the heels of her slender hands to her forehead, her blond hair scattering around her shoulders like sunlight, looking as lovely as a hymn *and* looking as if she had just received some very bad news.

Uh-oh. Panic bit him. He sat up straighter in his chair, fearing the worst. Maybe he had better pray that he could piece it together from whatever Pastor Mark said next.

"Lucky dog," Jason Huntley leaned close to whisper. "I thought you were just going to supervise like last year. I would roll up my sleeves if it meant spending time with Lucy."

Spending time with Lucy? His panic ramped up a notch. Yes, that was exactly what scared him. He followed the direction of Jason's nod—to Lucy, of course. A terrible sense of foreboding settled like a fist in his stomach. Whatever rolling up his sleeves meant, he wasn't going to like it.

He watched as Lucy lowered her hands from her face, and her green gaze fixed on his. She gave a little helpless shrug, and his heart turned over. Just like that.

He ripped his gaze away from hers, fighting panic, and fighting the words he would not let himself acknowledge. The unspoken truth remained lodged in his chest waiting, just waiting to be brought out into the open.

You do not like her, he told himself stubbornly although it was too late.

The rest of the meeting was a blur. He kept dreading the moment when he would have to walk through the conference room, down the hall and out to his truck, trying to avoid Lucy all that way. Knowing his luck, it would never happen. His problems around her had only gotten worse. He couldn't concentrate on the business at hand—thank the Lord his part was already done. Everywhere he looked, she was somehow in his line of sight, sitting serenely at the table with her hands folded, listening attentively and looking so beautiful his teeth hurt—or maybe that was because he was grinding them.

Who was he kidding? He had more than a secret crush on her, and he was headed down a dangerous path. He liked her very much. How could he not? She was like looking at sunshine in winter, like decorations on a Christmas tree. She made his stony heart hurt whenever she smiled. What was he going to do about that?

The solution was obvious. He had to go back to staying away from her, but considering he had just agreed to work with her on the project, that meant one of them would have to quit. He wasn't a quitter—not by a long shot. So that meant it would have to be Lucy.

You aren't going to ask me to step down, are you? Her words came back to him. Remembering how she had stood before him, just a little thing with frail feelings soft on her face made his heart roll over.

Somehow he would have to get her to change her mind. Maybe now that she knew they would be working together, she would be ecstatic to change, jubilant. He could always hope.

"We'll see you all next week," Pastor Mark said as if from a distance, and almost everyone around the table was standing.

Spence hopped to his feet, feeling a step behind everyone else. Friendly conversations rose to fill the room. He had a dozen or more things he could say to anyone standing around him, but did he? No. His attention went to Lucy.

She was chatting with Pastor Mark, kindness shining through her like dawn. He strained to hear a snippet of Lucy's gentle alto. "I am very committed to the children's wing. This is a fine thing the church is doing providing Christmas for the kids. I know how much that means to families torn between the hospital and home."

"We try to reach out to those in their time of need, whether they are believers or not," Pastor Mark went on to say.

Spence grabbed his briefcase and marched toward the door. Nothing had ever been so hard as deliberately walking away from Lucy. She was supposed to be flaky, some artist type who cared only for herself and getting attention. Except her sincerity rang in his ears, and although he didn't want to, he knew the sound of truth when he heard it.

I know how much that means to families torn between the hospital and home. Her voice was stuck on Play, and it looped over and over again. He couldn't get it to stop. Maybe his conscience wouldn't let him.

He hit the main hall and kept going. He didn't look right or left. He nodded at a few folks he knew as he passed by them but didn't pause to talk. The image of Lucy at Katherine's sink with sorrow on her face and tears in her eyes battered him. Did that mean she had gone through some kind of loss?

"Spence!"

Lucy. He recognized her voice, since his brain seemed to have recorded it. He steeled himself to face her. The hallway was loud with conversations and folks milling around near the beverage station, but his gaze went right to her hurrying toward him, her hair flying, with a file folder in hand and her coat bunched over one arm. The only words that came to mind were, *you are so beautiful.*

Good thing his throat had seized up. He mentally grimaced. As if he could say that to her.

"We need to talk." She smelled like sweet lilacs and gentle sunshine and sugar cookies. She looked like heaven smiling.

A tiny drop of tenderness sprang to life in his stony, barren heart, and he did his best to beat it out. Why her? Why did it have to be for her?

Chapter Eight

Lucy almost didn't mind that Spence scowled at her with unmistakable distaste. She didn't care if he didn't like her. None of it mattered. He had volunteered to do all he could for the kids. She hugged the file folder to her. She loved those kids. Okay, any kid.

"Let's duck in here." He opened a classroom door and held it. "We can talk without being disturbed."

"Good idea." The hallway was pretty noisy. Not that she was eager to be alone with him, but it couldn't be avoided. Their footsteps echoed in the room, and she set her things on the nearest desk. What was the best way to handle this situation? She was stuck working with Spence. A wise girl would make the best of it and manage to keep him a good distance away in case he decided to bring out the harsh comments again.

The door shut hard, echoing in the room. Spence looked troubled and a million miles away. "I'm surprised by this as much as you are."

"I'm touched that you want to make a difference. I didn't know you had it in you."

"I deserve that." He hung his head.

"No, I meant that as a compliment." It wasn't as if she admired him or anything, but he did have some very admirable qualities. "Everyone is talking about how you never get involved. But that's different now. You must really believe in this project."

"Uh, sure." There he went, looking uncomfortable again.

Heaven knew what he was thinking. She didn't want to look *too* friendly. He seemed to be uncomfortable with that, too. "I know it couldn't have been easy volunteering, especially after what happened."

"Sometimes I'm too harsh." He stared at the ground between them. A muscle jerked along his jawline.

"So, you have one flaw."

That made him smile a little. "I hate to break it to you, but I have more than one."

"Sure, I didn't want to point them all out."

"Thanks. I appreciate that." Now he was really smiling, inside and out.

"Any time. As long as you don't start pointing out all my flaws."

"It's a deal." He pulled out a chair and folded himself into it. He watched her carefully. "I hear you volunteer a lot. Why the hospital?"

She went perfectly still. She didn't move for a full fifteen seconds, each one ticking by slower than the last. Her face shadowed. "I don't know you enough to tell you that."

He winced. "I deserve that. But you can trust me, Lucy. I've got my flaws, but I know how to keep a confidence."

"It's very private." Tension dug into her face, etching fine lines at the corners of her eyes and around her mouth—lines of great pain.

Uncertainty cinched around his chest, making it tough to breathe. Maybe he didn't want to know what haunted Lucy. Everyone had pain. He had pain and he didn't particularly want to look at it or anyone else's. No good came from it.

Or at least, that's how he usually handled things. So why did he want to know? It was like a thirst in his soul, and he waited, wondering about the woman who slid behind the desk, using the surface cluttered with her things and the distance between them like a shield.

It was the real Lucy Chapin, he realized. The sunshine was gone and so was the cute smile. She sat quietly, looking very different from the perky blond who was always upbeat. There was a deeper layer to her, and he felt the pull of it on his well-defended heart.

"The man I was engaged to had a four-year-old son who was diagnosed with leukemia ten days before our wedding." Her eyes silvered, but no tears fell. "Of course we canceled the wedding."

He nodded once in acknowledgment. It was the most he could muster. Pain exploded through him as he realized what he had said. That afternoon in the kitchen mocked him. *What was wrong with him? Didn't he have enough money?*

He bowed his head, unable to fathom what he had done. No wonder she had dropped the dish. How could she stand to look at him at all? Heaven knew he couldn't stand himself.

He took a gulp of air, surprised he could actually speak. "I'm s-sorry, Lucy. I didn't know."

"I know you didn't." She did understand. He could see that plainly. She held no ill will toward him when she had every right to. The sorrow written on her face tortured him.

"You don't need to say anymore." He stood up, making enough noise to drown out the thoughts in his head that would not go away. Leukemia. There had never been a wedding. He knew the little boy she had loved had died.

He thought of Dorrie and how she had enough heart to love another woman's children as much as her own. That's the way Lucy had been. He could see it. He shoved the chair back in place. The legs scraping against the tile sounded like his soul crying out. Some things were too painful to think about.

He wasn't wrong a lot, but this time was a whopper. He had judged Lucy at every turn, so harshly, so un-Christian-like, because of his own fears, because of his own feelings. He was afraid if he didn't, then he would care for her even more.

Too late. She stood in his highest esteem, and after all he had done, she couldn't stand him. He deserved that.

"I know what those families are going through." She said simply through a veil of tears, her chin set and all pure strength. For a petite thing, fragile and gentle-hearted, she was steel, too. "It's the reason I left Portland. In the end, the memories were too hard. Only Pastor Marin knows this about me."

"Understood. I'll keep this private."

"Thank you." She wiped her eyes, trying to smile. "Look at me. I'm a mess. Now you really are thinking twice about working with me. Remember you said you don't go back on your word?"

He saw what she was doing, tucking away the things that hurt. He took her coat and shook it out, holding it for her. "It's tempting, but I won't fire you. You have all the notes."

"Whew." She turned and slipped into the coat.

Tenderness spilled into his heart, one miserly drop at a time—tenderness he couldn't hold back.

"We'll need to get together." She stepped away, hugging the coat to her as if for comfort. "We should make it as painless as possible for us both. I know I'm not your favorite person."

"I've never said that."

"Actions speak louder than words." She didn't meet his gaze as she hooked her purse over her shoulder.

Direct hit. "Let's face it, I've been awful to you."

"Yes, you have. And for your information, I didn't know Katherine had been trying to fix me up with you when I first moved here. It hadn't been my idea."

"I'm not your first choice of a man, sure." He deserved that, too. It was the story of his life.

"No, I wasn't in a position to think about dating again. Katherine didn't know that."

"I didn't either." Heat stained his face. He had never felt more shamed or embarrassed around anyone. "It's what I do, Lucy. If there's the slightest chance of a woman being interested in me, I make sure to stop it. It wasn't anything personal."

"It feels personal, Spence. Take some advice." The shadows were in her eyes again as she laid her hand on his arm.

The tenderness within him doubled against his will. He tried to swallow and couldn't. He tried to move away and couldn't. He was held in place by the connection of her simple touch.

"You're making a habit of pushing people away and closing them out." Earnest and sincere, all caring, came her words. She walked away in slow, measured steps. His arm felt cold where she had touched him. "One day all you will have is a heart too hard to love anyone and no one who loves you in return. Trust me. I know."

How? he wondered. How did she know? He watched, speechless in amazement, as she pulled open the door and disappeared into the hall. There was too much residual noise to make out the pad of her footsteps walking away from him.

He picked up the file folder she had forgotten. How had she known his worst fears? He rushed out into the hall, but there was no sign of her. A handful of people from the meeting were clustered together, sipping tea. A few of them turned to him and nodded in acknowledgment.

Jason Huntley gave him a thumbs-up. They all probably thought he had volunteered to help Lucy because he was sweet on her.

They didn't know the half of it.

"How did the meeting go?" Danielle asked the second he walked in the bookstore.

"Tolerable." He scowled, sending one of the new hires scurrying. He scowled harder as the door swung shut with a tinkle of the overhead bell. He hadn't meant to frighten the help. "Can't you find someone less skittish?"

"Brother dear, it would take Attila the Hun not to quake when you look like that." Danielle went up on tiptoe. He winced, and she wrapped her arms around him.

He didn't hug her back. He wanted to, but how would that look? People would stop scattering when he frowned. The next thing he knew, he would have to start talking about his feelings. He rolled his eyes and put one arm around his sister in a half hug. Then he broke away. "That's enough. This is a place of business."

"How inappropriate of me." She rolled her eyes, not offended, trying not to laugh at him.

She had his number, all right. He was fairly fond of her. He kept his frown in place and marched toward the cash registers.

"How did the meeting go?"

"It was a meeting." He rounded the counter, refusing to give up any more information. The cashier, their cousin, Kelly, looked up from her textbook and gave him a smile. She was back from California, married and in graduate school now. There was a sensible girl. She never quaked when he stormed by. He tossed her a smile, careful that no one else saw it, as he stalked toward his office.

"That's it? It was just a meeting?" Dani was smiling by the sound of it as she brushed past his desk and settled into one of the armchairs by the window. "I expected something more informative. Maybe even a show of your temper?"

"I know why you stepped down from being the committee chair." He dropped his briefcase beneath his desk and shucked off his overcoat. "You wanted Lucy to take your place."

"I suppose that is one consequence." Her eyes twinkled at him. "Morning sickness might be the real motive here."

He knew Danielle. She would never hurt him intentionally. But she was one of the few who had found a happy and loving marriage, one without deceit and worse, and so she looked at marriage through a serious set of rose-colored glasses. "You meant well, but do you want to know what happened?"

"I'm dying of curiosity." She leaned forward in her chair.

"I'm the committee head in your place." He tossed his coat over the file cabinet and paused for effect. "Me."

"You?" She bit her bottom lip and choked.

"You're laughing."

"Who me? No, I'm not laughing."

"Because you're fighting it." He wasn't fooled. It really was funny. He dropped into his chair. There was no way he was going to admit how it happened. That was strictly private information. "Go ahead and laugh. I deserve it."

"Something tells me you are going to love getting involved." Danielle leaned back in the chair and crossed her ankles, looking as if she were already picturing the outcome.

Oh, he knew what she was thinking. He scowled harder. "I'm not going to wind up with Lucy. She can't stand me."

"Lucy is warm and wonderful. She loves everyone."

"Not me. I can guarantee that." He thought of the sadness he had caused her, what she must think of him. He tapped his keyboard, and the computer screen blinked on. "Let's go over your schedule."

"Why? You're not replacing me already, are you?"

"No, but you *are* cutting back on your work hours. That's an executive order." All he had to do was think of Katherine with her feet up lying in bed all day, trying to combat high blood pressure. He should have taken a firmer hand with her and refused to let her work the instant she had told him about her pregnancy. Working hadn't caused the problem, but it hadn't helped it. "Your only job will be finding and training your replacement."

"Spence, you can't manage everything on your own."

"I can handle it. What I can't handle is worrying you will lose the baby." His voice sounded strained, and he hated that he had tipped his hand toward his emotions like that. He would have to give Katherine a call in a bit and make sure she didn't need him to do anything for her. She had a husband, a teenaged stepdaughter and sisters ready to run at a moment's notice, but he had his responsibility, too. "I mean it, Danielle. If you argue, then you are out of here today."

"Spence, you are being unreasonable. Again." Gently spoken, she launched out of the chair and came his way.

He sure hoped she wasn't going to hug him. He didn't approve of affection. Okay, maybe he did, but it embarrassed him. He held out his hand, hoping that would stop her. It slowed her down.

"I don't know what I'm going to do with you." She sat on the edge of his desk and ruffled his hair. "You're hopeless."

"I know. And I sort of care about you."

"I sort of care about you, too." She didn't hug him.

Whew. He relaxed and turned to his computer. "You're coming in late from now on. No arguing. We have to account for morning sickness. If it's troubling you, then you stay home."

"I sailed through my other two pregnancies with just a little stomach upset."

"You can't be too careful." As he adjusted the scheduling, he thought of what Lucy had told him. Four years old. He remembered Dani's son at that age. Tyler had loved fire trucks and the color red and playing with the garden hose for hours. He still did. What had Lucy's stepson-to-be been like? Precious, that's what. Every child was precious.

"No more working evenings." He deleted her from the schedule. "Too bad Lauren is managing Gran's commercial properties, or she could take over for you."

"I'll talk to her and see if she has any suggestions," Danielle offered. "She might know someone."

"And put an ad in the paper." He tried to concentrate but his thoughts kept returning to Lucy and the broken dish in the sink and the blood dripping from her hand. He also thought about the quiet solemn layers of her depth and compassion.

"Are you all right, Spence?" Dani sounded far away.

He nodded his head. No. He wasn't all right. He was never going to be all right again. It wouldn't be all right with Lucy Chapin walking around in the world able to pop into the bookstore at any minute, able to see right to the core of him where no one was allowed.

"I'm fine," he said, touched that Danielle cared. But could he show it? No.

Lucy was right. It was a serious habit with him to push people away and close them out. He was doing it right now with his sister and he trusted her. He rubbed his hand across his forehead. Thinking of Lucy was making his brain hurt.

"You don't look fine." Danielle and her persistent gentle care would not relent. "You haven't looked okay for almost two weeks. Since Thanksgiving. I know everyone was really pressuring you."

"Pressuring me? You all had me practically engaged."

"We were just hoping, that is all." Her caring was a given. She had always been that way—would always be.

He could count on his family's love for him. He might not be able to accept it, and he might not be able to show it, but they were always going to be there even if their lives were changing. Not needing him anymore. He cleared his throat. "I know you were all spying when I was in the kitchen with Lucy."

"You were holding her hand. We were all peeking around the dining room archway watching you."

He couldn't stand to look at her. All her hopes for him would be shining there and her beliefs in him. She didn't know what he had done. Ashamed, he couldn't speak. He remembered the loss dark in Lucy's eyes and her wise words. Had she been lost in despair? Had she lost her heart, too? Pain could do that to a person. He knew. He figured loss could, too.

"I heard through the grapevine that you dug out Lucy's car and drove it home for her." Danielle was using her understanding tone, as if she had it all figured out. "Volunteering with her will be a good chance for you to get to know her. Promise me something."

"No." He tapped the keyboard and saved the file. "No promises."

"Follow your heart. I know you have one." She smiled at him. "It might be as shrunken and as black as a piece of coal, but you have one."

He rolled his eyes. "Will you be quoting Dr. Seuss to me next?"

"Either that or Charles Dickens." She swung off the desk and opened his door. "I'll go write an ad for the paper, Ebenezer."

"I'm not a scrooge," he argued, but she was already gone, breezing around the corner to her office.

Kelly startled out of her reading, looked up and glanced over her shoulder. "You're not a scrooge, Spence. Mostly."

"Thanks for the reassurance." Did everyone have to kid him today of all days? He went back to his desk. He felt raw inside, and Lucy had everything to do with it.

"It's Dorrie on line one for you, Ebenezer." Danielle's smiling voice came over the intercom.

"I'm not a scrooge." What was with everyone these days? They had gotten cheeky—a terrible side effect of happiness. He snatched up the phone. "Hi, Dorrie. What can I do for you?"

"I just heard the news. I'm proud of you, sweetie."

He grimaced. He loved Dorrie, but he was no longer thirteen years old. He was a grown man and had a reputation to protect. If only he could set her straight on the "sweetie" part. He had better just ignore it. "I accidentally volunteered to help with a Christmas project."

"So you will be busy for part of Christmas. You tell me when you're available so I can work our family feast around it."

That couldn't be why she was calling, right? "Great. I'll let you know. Is there something up? What can I do for you? Dad isn't having problems with that right front tire again, is he?"

"Oh, no, nothing like that. I just wanted to talk to my boy." Dorrie sounded like she was one of those hot air balloons floating over the city.

It was Lucy, he realized. Of course, she had jumped to conclusions about Lucy. He launched out of his chair, taking the cordless phone with him and staring out at the snow berms in the parking lot. "Whatever you are thinking about me and Lucy, delete it."

"But Spence, I've started to hope all over again."

"Don't. You'll just be disappointed." He did his best to stay gruff, but he had a soft spot for his stepmother. "You heard Lucy. What nice woman is going to want me? If you want to marry me off, you will have to find a woman looking for a curmudgeon for a husband."

"What kind of woman would that be? She might be pretty hard to find."

"That's the idea."

Dorrie started to laugh. "Oh you, you had me going there for a minute. I'll have you know that I'm praying for you as hard as I can."

"Good. Then a woman who might be looking for a man in his mid-thirties who is sweet on his ma will be coming along any second."

"Oh, you aren't sweet on me."

"In a distant, fond sort of way."

"I love you too, Spence. When you see Lucy, you say hi from me." Dorrie's loving voice was warm and smiling again.

Why was everyone so happy? Spence rolled his eyes. It wasn't sensible to live like that. Just reckless, that's what. Not something he could do. You never knew when and how life was going to disappoint you. Best to keep expectations low so you weren't sideswiped.

He disconnected and stared out the window. Lucy. All he had to do was think her name, and tenderness winked into existence like blinking Christmas lights. They were everywhere inside the store. Danielle and Kelly had gone nuts with the Christmas decorations. Personally, he thought Christmas hymns over the speaker system were enough.

I'm not a scrooge, he told himself, and if a tiny voice in his soul wanted to argue, he soundly ignored it.

Lucy looked up from her screen to the haze of twilight darkening the forest outside her window. Her head hurt from trying to think too hard, and her heart ached from a day of trying not to feel too much. That's what happened whenever she came face-to-face with the past. It was best to keep those memories buried if she could.

Bean landed with a loud cat thump on the edge of

her desk. The Persian flicked her tail once and gave an admonishing meow.

"Is it that time already?" She rubbed her eyes. Her vision was blurry from staring at the screen while she wrote and rewrote two pages all afternoon long. Work had been a disaster today. She should have known better than to try to write. Maybe tomorrow would be more productive.

She saved her file and closed her laptop. "In case you get any ideas," she told the furry feline as she rubbed the cat's ears. "I know you hate the computer."

Although Bean understood English perfectly well, she offered an innocent look. The ten-pound cat had mysteriously managed to break three keyboards over the years.

"C'mon, cutie. I'll refill your bowl." Lucy eased out of her chair with a creak, she really had been sitting too long, and a flash of light caught her attention.

Headlights came down her driveway. Strange, since she wasn't expecting anyone and not many people visited her way out in the boonies. The lights were coming closer, and she recognized the green pickup that parked in front of her garage.

Spence McKaslin.

Chapter Nine

She could see him plainly through the windshield. He was the only man she knew who could frown like that and still look gorgeous. Maybe it was the thick fall of his brown hair that softened his harsh features or the rugged, striking cut of his face. Maybe it was his masculine presence that radiated goodness and decency. Whatever it was, she should not be noticing.

His door swung open and he climbed out. He was going to come to the door. Of course, that only made sense, but suddenly it was a reality. She was going to have to open the door and face him. Like this. Yikes! Her reflection in the glass wall of windows stared back at her.

She groaned. I look like a bag lady, she thought, cringing. She wore her glasses instead of her contacts. She had pulled her hair back in a ponytail, and who knew what it was doing? It was probably sticking straight out. Her gray sweats were baggy and had a hole in one knee. They were her most comfy writing pants, and it wasn't as if anyone was around to see her...usually.

Why did it have to be Spence? What she would give
for time to change. She dashed through the house flick-
ing on lights. Since she hadn't closed the blinds yet, she
had a perfect view of him striding with athletic grace
up the front steps. He was carrying something—she
couldn't seem to focus on it. It was the look he wore that
drew and kept her attention like a supercharged mag-
net. He wasn't scowling any longer. He wasn't frowning. She didn't think she had ever seen that expression
on his face before. It was a little like kindness.

Oh, no. She skidded to a stop, heart pounding with
dread. She could handle his frown. She was prepared
for his scowling demeanor. She could even take the
troubled Spence she had seen earlier today. But a kind
Spence McKaslin was something she couldn't handle.
Was it too late to pretend she wasn't home?

He rapped on the window—not the door. Startled
out of her thoughts, she realized he had spotted her. Too
late. There was nothing left to do but face the music
and Spence McKaslin. She watched him nod and point
toward her door.

She nodded. Yes, she would let him in. She dragged
her feet forward. The worst had already happened. Not
only did he know about the sorest spot in her soul, something terribly private and painful, but he had seen her
like this. At least it couldn't get worse. She said a quick
prayer, braced herself and opened the door.

"Sorry to drop by like this." The big man towered po-
litely on her doorstep with a baby Christmas tree tucked
in one arm and a file folder clutched in his other hand.
"I needed to say something to you, and I didn't want to
say it over the phone."

Icy air breezed right through her and she shivered.

It was too cold to make him stand outside. "Come in. I'll make us some tea."

"I'd appreciate it."

She backed up so he could enter, aware of his masculine presence in her domain. Something about him tugged at her spirit. Something about him made her want to be the kind of girl who could start dreaming again. Her dreams were fictional these days and nothing more. She closed the door. "Let me take your coat."

"First this." He held out the live tree. "This is for you."

"For me?" That seemed unlikely. The adorable little fir was decorated with a single string of tiny white lights, a golden garland and silver and gold ornaments. A delicate glass angel was lashed to the top, breathtakingly beautiful. She had seen the ornaments in the McKaslins' bookstore. Had he taken the time to decorate the tree himself?

No, she couldn't picture it. One of his sisters probably did or maybe an employee. "I don't understand."

"I made you sad twice now. I would have brought flowers, but Danielle has been calling me Ebenezer, so—" He shrugged. "I brought a little bit of Christmas instead."

He pushed the ceramic pot holding the tree into her hands. She saw another new emotion on his face, one of deepest sincerity. "I'm sorry, Lucy. I said the wrong thing today."

"You made me remember the past, that's all."

"I reminded you of an unbearable loss. And I don't want to do it again. So don't think about it. Think about how much you can't stand me." He smiled.

Wow, Spence was incredibly handsome when he smiled. She nearly dropped the pot in surprise. She stared, smiling right along with him, noticing there were midnight flecks of darker blue in his deep blue eyes. She couldn't help sighing just a tiny bit.

"I can't stand you only a little," she confessed, kidding him. "What is it the twins say? A pinch. A dash. A smidgeon, or something like that."

"Something like that." He unzipped his coat. "What's with your cat?"

"My cat?" Normally Bean kept her distance from strangers. It was the feline's opinion that other humans were highly suspicious creatures. So why was she rubbing her cheek against Spence's jeans leg? "I don't think that's my cat. I think it's a weird alien clone."

"I don't approve of cats." Spence scowled again.

This time she caught the flicker of humor in his captivating eyes. He really was more bark than bite. She carefully carried the tree into the house with her. "I don't approve of cats either."

"I can see that because she is so abused." He followed her, carefully sidestepping the persistent animal. "I see two cat condos."

"I don't approve of cat condos," she quipped.

"And blankets on the couch cushions."

"I don't know who put those there." She set the tree on the kitchen table. "Some phantom cat lover."

"I especially don't approve of those." He *almost* couldn't keep frowning. She really was pretty funny— a little quirky, but funny. And her house wasn't what he expected at all. He expected a big fancy house with showy pieces instead of a smaller place with cozy, comfortable furniture. Bookshelves, as far as he could see, lined the walls of every room, including the kitchen.

"You don't approve of a lot of things." She took his

coat and hung it over the back of one of the kitchen chairs.

"It's intentional." He admired the wall of books where most women might put a hutch. "If I started approving of everything, then what would happen to my reputation?"

"I see your point. People might start actually liking you." She was smiling. It wasn't an admonishment.

She understood him. It had been a long time since anyone had. He was on unfamiliar ground. He didn't know what to do, but he did know that whatever he said, he had better say it with care. He was not going to make her sad a third time. He laid the folder on the counter. "This is yours. You left it behind in the church."

"Oh, I hadn't realized. Thanks. I suppose we will need that." She opened a cabinet door, revealing boxes and boxes of all kinds of tea. "Any preferences?"

"You pick." He didn't care. He doubted any of the variety of flavors on that shelf would ease the tension in his jaw joints. He tried to relax and couldn't. Why did Lucy make him tense? It was a mystery of the universe.

"How about Joyful Holidays?" She pulled down a box decorated with Christmas ornaments and holly. "Fitting, don't you think? I assume you want to talk about the file folder, now that you're here."

"I didn't look in it."

She looked surprised as she lifted a rumbling tea kettle from the professional-grade stove. "The folder is nothing personal. It's my shopping list for the kids."

"Shopping list? Isn't that a last minute kind of thing?" He flipped open the folder and scanned the neatly organized list of businesses and individuals and what they had donated in prior years. "I mean, you don't know who is going to be in the hospital until the last minute, right?"

"In many ways, yes." She filled two big ceramic cups with hot water. "There are a certain amount of children we know will be in the ward for Christmas."

He served in an executive capacity on the board; he had gone over the requests for funds and approved plans and proposals. He had never taken the time to give much thought to the children their church helped. As he turned the page, he saw a write-up on one of the kids—three-year-old Ashlinn Thomas, who had been diagnosed with cancer two days before Thanksgiving. He stared at the digital picture of a blond-haired, brown-eyed little munchkin with dimples and the sweetest smile.

He hung his head. His problems evaporated like morning mist. His niece, Madison, would turn three the day after Christmas. He closed the folder, unable to look anymore.

"Do you want to come into the TV room?" She carried two mugs with her as she walked away from him. "It's really a family room, but as it's only me here it seems weird to call it a family room."

"I know what you mean. I have one of those, too." He had put one in the house he had built five years ago as an investment. It was two minutes from Katherine's house, five from Danielle's and four blocks from his parent's townhouse. Work was less than a five-minute drive if he hit all the lights.

Anyone could see that Lucy's house was a home. There were personal things like an apple-shaped vase on the fireplace mantel and a row of family pictures in shadow boxes marching along the top of the bookshelves. The books were everything from classics to history to political biographies to inspirational fiction. Sort of like his at home.

He followed her to the comfortable furniture partly facing the fireplace and a wide screen. He had to keep looking down to avoid the cat, which kept trying to trip him.

"Bean, stop that." Lucy rolled her eyes. "I don't know what has gotten into her. It must be your masculine charm."

"I wasn't aware I had any."

"Maybe it's only detectable to cats?" Her eyes were laughing at him.

"That would explain why I can't get any dates." That wasn't the reason, but it felt good to laugh with her. He settled into one of the overstuffed chairs, which was even more comfortable than it looked, and took his mug off the central coffee table where Lucy had set it. The cat leaped up onto the arm and knocked her cheek against his shoulder.

"Maybe I should put Bean outside." Lucy came close, bringing with her the scent of lilacs and sunshine. She scooped the furry feline off the chair arm and cradled the cat like a baby. She walked to the nearest French door and gently set her feline outside. The Persian flicked her tail several times and stalked off, looking very perturbed.

"I'm in big trouble for that, but she would have made you spill your tea." Lucy dropped into the chair across from him and put her stocking feet on the coffee table. She wrapped her hands around the ceramic cup and sipped. "Don't worry. It's cold out there, but she has a kitty door around back."

"Bean?" he asked.

"Strange name, I know. When she was a kitten, she

didn't walk, she hopped. She used to bounce around like a Mexican jumping bean. So it stuck."

"She's more like Velcro now?"

"Exactly. Except with the name Bean, there are endless puns."

"I know I'm going to regret asking. Puns?"

"When I come home, I can say, where have you bean?" She blushed a little. Cute. Real cute. "If she's been sleeping in the dryer I can say, careful, don't turn into a baked bean. Corny, I know, but I live alone. I have to amuse myself."

"I live alone, and I don't amuse myself."

"Pardon me, Spence, but you don't approve of amusement. Don't deny it. I know you were thinking it."

He laughed. What he was thinking, was that she was captivating in the pure, innocent way of snow falling from a midnight sky or dawn's soft glow in midwinter.

Tenderness filled him as he gazed upon her. Her round glasses made her look like a bookworm, but then he was partial to bookworms. Her hair was pulled back in a haphazard ponytail, off-center and all manner of silken strands had fallen down to riot around her face. How a woman could look more beautiful in baggy, mostly worn-out sweats than in designer clothes he didn't know, but he could not look away.

"Okay, so I might have been thinking it. I don't approve of a lot of things, except hard work," he said, intending to sound gruff. But did it work? No. Lucy had somehow stolen his gruffness.

"I agree with you. Hard work is one ingredient to a happy life." She didn't blink, and to his shock, she was agreeing with him.

Yes, it would have been much better if he could have resisted coming.

"So, do you want to go over the files, since you're here?" She took a long sip of her tea, watching him over the rim.

"Might as well. I'm not imposing on you?"

"No. My work day is done, and as you can see, I have a lot going on here, but I think I can squeeze you into my jam-packed evening schedule."

Behind her, the uncovered windows reflected the room and his own face staring besotted at her. You are *not* falling for Lucy Chapin, he ordered himself sternly, praying it would work. It was the only defense he had left around her. If he couldn't count on his self-discipline, then he was in big trouble.

She forked the last bite of oriental chicken salad and tried to convince herself she wasn't disappointed the evening was coming to an end. His stay had been a pleasant one. While she had filled him in on all that had been done and what was left to do before their big Christmas party, she had pulled out the bowl of salad she had made the night before and toasted thick chunks of French bread in the oven. They had sat down at the table to go over the kids on their list so far. Now, the meal was done and they had reached the last child in the folder. Timothy Lyman.

She watched Spence as he studied the computer printed page. She had met Timothy and taken his picture earlier in the week. Although the seven-year-old boy had fractured half the bones in his body in a car accident, he still managed to make a funny face for her camera.

"He wants to be a fireman." Spence rubbed a hand over his face. "So does my nephew."

She thought of how hard the world could be and took

the folder. "These children need Christmas. It's hope. It's joy. It's a moment in time where they can forget about their illnesses and injuries and just be little kids again…where they can be reminded of God's love for them."

He nodded. "I don't know why I'm here. You know what you're doing, Lucy. You should be chairing this, not me."

"Are you abandoning me?" She knew he wasn't, but it made him grin.

"I'm not the kind of man who jumps ship—ever. Believe me, I'm not trying to get out of this. I don't have anything to offer. I don't think I am the man for the job."

"Why do you say that?"

"I'm good at running things and juggling projections and goals and budgets. I'm excellent at telling people what to do."

"I have three volunteers. You can boss them around."

"Oh boy." He rubbed a hand over his forehead. "I'm afraid this requires more than what I've got."

She started to argue with him, but he meant what he said. He genuinely did. For a moment, he looked bleak. He had the kind of sadness that made her catch her breath.

Hopelessness. She knew the look and the feel of it. She had once walked that dark place. She laid her hand on his. He was like sun-warmed marble, strong and impossibly human. "I think you are exactly right for this project."

"You mean you need someone to boss you around?"

"Nice try, big fella, but humor isn't going to work. You need to learn to take a compliment." She liked him. Heaven help her, she really did. "Everyone brings something different to this. To the world. You do the best with what you've got. It will be enough."

"It's more than finding presents for some kids. I can see that right now." He looked troubled, as if he did not believe her.

"Everything good in life always requires more than it seems." Gentle feelings swept through her. "You're enough, Spence. You really are."

His throat worked, and he looked away. It was hard to tell if she had said what he needed to know or if she had said too much. He remained silent and she withdrew her hand, wishing she could withdraw her words as easily. She pushed away from the table and from the big stoic man sitting, but he filled the room with amazing presence. Spence was a tough man to ignore.

"Did your cut heal up?"

She saw his reflection in the windows as she put the rest of the bread loaf away. "It's just fine."

"Good. You wouldn't want to get an infection."

"No." She sensed what he was really asking her. And it had nothing to do with the injury to her hand but about the single truth he knew about her.

She capped the ginger salad dressing and returned it to the refrigerator door. "It's not easy being reminded of Christian, but I believe in the work I do. It's his memory I serve."

"You don't have to talk about it." He rose from the chair, all six feet-plus. "I didn't want to remind you."

"I know. I'm reminded of him every day. It never goes away." While it could make her sad, the memory warmed her heart, too. The bond she and a little boy shared still lived. It still mattered. It made a difference. She made sure of it. "I never want to forget him. I never want to live in a world where a little boy's love is something that is best forgotten."

Spence swiped the back of his neck, looking unmoved as he paced toward her, towering above her like granite. It was not ice she saw on his face or stone in his heart. "Just when I think I can't like you anymore, you go and say something like that. I don't want to like you, Lucy."

"I don't want to like you, Spence, but I do." Heaven help her. It wasn't a mistake, was it? "Do you want dessert? I picked up some sugar cookies from Ava's bakery on the way home."

"Thanks, but I had better go. It's getting late."

"The roads are probably already freezing. I should have thought of it sooner."

"I have snow tires and four-wheel drive."

He was a very good driver, she knew, under any conditions. Spence McKaslin radiated a steady capability that was deeply attractive, too. Just add that to his other fine qualities—more things she had to try not to notice. She mentally rolled her eyes. Sure, like that was possible.

"It looks as if you and I are going to be spending a lot of time together." Was that a hint of a smile?

Yes. She definitely wasn't imagining it. She pulled a red plastic gift baggie from the box in the drawer and carried it to the bakery box on the breakfast bar. "You're right. We have to spend lots of time together. Organizing lists. Calling donors and retailers. Wrapping presents. I hope your gift wrapping skills are top-notch."

"I'm no slacker."

No, Spence was the kind of man who did everything right. She opened the box and slipped a few cookies into the baggie.

"I guess we'll have to trade numbers." He sounded casual, as if it were nothing but business.

So why did her heart skip three beats? Why did her spirit brighten just a bit? There was no logical reason. Spence was not the kind of man she was looking for.

On another hand, he was exactly what she had been praying for. She handed him a pen and notepad she found in the top drawer. "How about your e-mail addy too? That way I can e-mail your half of the donor list to make calls from."

"Sure." He moved close, writing away. His head was bent, his dark hair tumbled across his brow and his deep blue eyes watched her, not the notepad. He clicked the pen and set it on top of the paper, his writing done. He towered over her close enough to touch, his gaze intense on hers.

Gulp. Her pulse stilled. Her soul silenced. The world melted away until there was only him making her broken dreams breathe as if with life.

He is not the man for you, Lucy, she reminded herself. It would be a mistake to fall for someone as closed off as Spence. She had made that mistake before, and all she had left of it were the broken pieces of those failed hopes.

"I suppose you'll be at my sister's shower on Saturday?" Spence hooked his coat off the back of the chair.

"That's the plan." She grabbed the to-go cookie bag and followed him toward the front door. "Not only did I receive a written invitation but eight phone calls inviting me personally."

"Eight. That's a suspicious number." He paused in the foyer to pull on his jacket. "That's the number of women in my family."

"Yes. Your grandmother's call was the sweetest."

"I can't imagine what she said to you." He blushed, and it only made him more handsome, if that was possible.

Not that she should be noticing. "I understand completely, so don't worry. She loves you."

"I know. It's hard to imagine anyone can."

"No, that's not true." Because she didn't dare say what she meant, she went for humor. "Like I've said, all we have to do is find you the right woman, someone whose top three desired qualities in a man are scowling, frowning and gruffness."

"That's what you think my top three qualities are?" He reached for the doorknob. "I'm falling down on the job. I'm going to have to work on improving my surly reputation."

There was a lot she wanted to say, like how his reputation was more than fine. She liked the man who cared deeply for his family, whose faith was stalwart and unshakable and who worked hard to do what he thought was right. But if she said those things, then he would worry that she was starting to *really* like him, which she was. Maybe it would be better if that was her little secret.

"Don't forget dessert." She handed him the to-go bag of Christmas tree cookies. "It will put you in the holiday spirit."

"I'm never in the holiday spirit. Just thought I should warn you." His fingers brushed hers as he took the bag.

A spark snapped to life in her soul. Shock rolled through her. She had never felt anything like it before. She wrapped her arms around her middle as he stepped out into the cold evening. Snow was tumbling from a black sky. Snow. She had no idea. It hadn't been in the forecast.

"I'll contact you soon," he said in a strained voice as he hesitated outside the pool of the porch light. "Good night, Lucy. Thank you."

He didn't move. It was too dark to see anything but a blend of shadowed movement at his ankles. Bean.

"Good night, Spence." She knelt to gather the cat into her arms, standing in the reach of the porch light.

Without another word, he moved away to become part of the shadows and the night.

Chapter Ten

His two-story house was dark and cold, veiled with snow and framed by darkness. As the truck idled in the driveway waiting for the garage door to crank open, he could see the glow of lights from the neighboring houses but not his. There would be no kids waiting for him, no warm smells of supper cooking and no pretty wife to welcome him home.

And you don't want there to be, he reminded himself.

The door was up, so he eased the truck into the garage, shaking his head. What was wrong with him? He felt melancholy and dissatisfied with his life, more so ever since he had left Lucy's house two nights ago. It was ridiculous. This is the life he wanted, the life he prayed for. In fact, this was the life he was grateful to God for every day. There was no one to hurt him, no one to rip out his heart and no one to leave with every penny in savings when the going got tough.

He cut the engine, grabbed his briefcase and climbed into the frigid air. He hit the garage button, thinking as he sorted through his keys. He had stayed late at the bookstore to accommodate Christmas shoppers, and if no family member called needing some kind of problem solved, he could get a head start on January's operating budget since he had put that off doing donor calls.

The moment he stepped through the door and hit the lights, his cell phone rang. He punched in the code to the security system before hauling his phone out of his pocket. A check of the screen told him it was Dorrie. Relieved, he answered. "Aren't you and Dad out doing the town on a Friday night?"

"We're waiting for you to join us." Dorrie's cheer was welcome on this bleak winter's evening.

"Funny." He dropped his briefcase on the counter and hung his keys on the wall peg by the back door. "I have tomorrow down on my calendar. Katherine's baby shower. I won't forget."

"That's not why I'm calling." Dorrie sounded too happy.

It probably had something to do with Lucy. He rolled his eyes. He had been putting up with this for days. He braced himself. There was nothing else he could do. This storm would pass—eventually. He loosened his tie and walked to the pantry shelves, trying to muster up energy to cook something.

"I stopped by today and did some cleaning and laundry." Dorrie went on cheerfully. "I left a casserole in your fridge. Just heat it in the oven at three fifty until the cheese bubbles."

Guilt overwhelmed him. Dorrie, as she always did, made his life easier, better. She was a good mom. "Thanks, I appreciate it. I had a long day."

"I know. Did you hear Dani's good news?"

"I haven't seen her today. She wasn't scheduled to work. She had more good news?"

"Jonas is cleared to start work by the new year. He'll

have to stay on a desk job, no exceptions, but isn't that wonderful? Oh, another thing. I called the store and talked with Kelly. I wanted to make sure she's coming tomorrow and that you will *let her off work*." Dorrie emphasized.

He yanked open the fridge. "Yes, and I was going to pay her for the hours. Graduate school is expensive."

"That's right. Even if she's happily married now, that doesn't mean we can't still watch out for her."

That's how he felt, too. Long ago Kelly had been engaged to their cousin, who had died before they had married. As he pulled out the casserole, he realized that had happened to Lucy, too. Ten days before her wedding. That meant Lucy's flowers had been ordered, her wedding dress had been fitted and ready and her honeymoon plans were finalized. That meant her hopes for happiness, which had to have been so high, were irrevocably shattered.

He had seen the memories of that time in her house. He set the casserole on the counter and turned on the oven. There had been a collage frame of pictures above the fireplace mantel where a little boy's face had smiled. He had spotted the popsicle stick castle on an end table, clearly a small child's work, and a child's watercolor painting hanging in the kitchen.

He ached, thinking of her loss.

"Spence? Yoo-hoo." Dorrie's voice interrupted him and brought him back into the kitchen.

He shook his head, hoping that would clear out the stray thoughts. He wasn't the type of man who had a lot of stray thoughts. "Sorry, my mind drifted."

"Don't tell me you are thinking about January's budget already. You work too hard, Spence. I have been telling you this for years. You need to relax more, and maybe then you will see that there's more to life than profit and loss statements."

"Wait a minute." He was seeing a theme here. Having eight women in the family had taught him to watch for this kind of thing early and nip it in the bud. "What's going on?"

"I worry about you, Ebenezer."

Great. Here it came. "I'm not a scrooge. I give heavily to Christmas charities. You know I do."

"That's not what I mean. You aren't stingy, Spence. You are a generous man. But you are miserly with your heart."

"What is that supposed to mean? I'm fine. My life is fine."

"Yes, but you keep this up, sweetheart, and you are going to miss the best things life has to offer you." All loving care, that was Dorrie, and her words were laced with it so gently that he could not get angry at her.

He wanted to be, though. He was tired, that's what he was, because instead of protesting and explaining how much he never wanted to get married, he thought of Lucy—how incredibly beautiful she was with her crooked ponytail and stray locks curling every which way. Also of how comfortable it had been sitting with her over a cup of tea and leftovers for dinner. He also thought of how alone he felt now, thinking of her.

"Don't you want to be loved, Spence? To have someone truly love you and to love them as deeply? What about children? You are a fantastic uncle, but I know you want kids of your own."

He squeezed his eyes shut briefly, refusing to think about that—about any of it. He told himself he didn't approve of noisy kids in his house with their sticky fingers. It was all a lie, and as wrong as it was, he had to tell it to himself to keep his defenses together.

"There are a lot of things I can live without." He scowled. Dorrie already knew this. "Like a wife figuring out she can't love me and running off with the savings. Like kids being destroyed by it. I don't believe in the fairy tale. Sorry."

"I'm sorry, too." She sounded so sad.

The oven beeped, saving him from feeling too much. He grabbed the dish and jammed it into the oven. The door slammed, and he set the timer. "I've got next month's budget to work on. Dorrie, I've got to go. Thanks for the casserole and for everything you do."

"You're welcome, dear."

He said goodbye as fast as he could, hating that he'd disappointed her…again. He loved her, he did. She knew trust didn't come easy for him, so why was she pushing like this?

He wandered into the family room, turning on lights as he went and sat down at the computer. The house felt lonely. He logged online. The scent from the oven strengthened, making his stomach grumble. Dorrie had made his favorite casserole, just as she often had since before she had married Dad.

It seemed forever ago. How many years? Spence hated to add them up as he tapped his password on the keyboard. Over twenty years, he realized with a start. Back then he had been a teenaged boy hurting in the worst way, and he hadn't wanted anything to do with the motherly, kind Dorrie.

But she had won him over with her constant devotion year in and year out, making his favorite dishes one after another until she had won his trust. It had taken a long time, he remembered, years, in fact. But in the end, she hadn't left. When she said she loved him, she meant it. She said she didn't need to chase dreams because her family was her dream.

He clicked the mouse and scanned his inbox. Lucy's address stood out from the others. He opened the e-mail without even thinking about it and her words scrawled across his screen.

We have thirteen days of shopping left before Christmas and counting down. How goes the donor list?

He hit Reply and started to type.

Good. I'm sure my list is longer than yours.

He had no sooner hit Send than a message popped on his screen. It was an instant message request from Lucy. She must be online.

Aren't you the competitive one? She'd written.

Yes, he typed. He could picture her sitting at her computer wearing another pair of ragged sweats and her hair every which way. He kept typing. How have you bean?

He imagined the pause was her laughing.

Busy, came her reply, but good. I'm hoping to persuade you to spend time with me.

I hope there's cookies involved. I'm going to need incentive.

You're not fooling me, Spence. I bet you hardly like cookies.

True, he thought. She had him pegged. Baked goods weren't the draw. No, he thought, as his mind evaporated. There were no thoughts, no to-do lists carefully categorized in his head and no rational logic. Just her. Images of her standing in her doorway surprised to see him. Of her holding the tree he'd decorated for her. Of her smiling up at him, just him. Those mental pictures made the walls around his heart buckle and rend.

You are not falling for her, he reminded himself.

Her message flashed on his screen. Aha! Silence. I knew it. You are suddenly overcome with the spirit of Christmas, and you are too stubborn to let anyone know it. Right?

Wrong, he thought, but what did he type? I don't approve of the spirit of Christmas.

And why did he type it? So he could imagine her laughing. He liked the way green glints appeared in her emerald eyes and how she tipped her head back, joy bubbling out of her.

You are a challenge, Spence. But one I am up for. I hope you are ready because I am going to show you the true meaning of Christmas.

Credit card debt? He typed.

Bah, humbug. I think Danielle is right about you.

He groaned. I'm not a scrooge.

I was sort of hoping you were. At the end of the story, Ebenezer lets love and joy into his heart.

No wonder I haven't read that book. Ebenezer is a softie. He hit Send, figuring that would make her laugh, too.

You are impossible. You need more help than I thought. I had better get busy.

Get in line. You aren't the only female who thinks that.

All the more reason to get to work on you. How does tomorrow after the shower sound?

Doable. I'll somehow manage to tolerate your company, he typed when he wished he could say, I can't wait to see you again.

Good night, Spence.

Good night. He hit Send and waited. A message flashed on his screen telling him she had signed off.

No, he couldn't wait to see her. For a few moments in time, she had transported him out of his empty life and made the lonesomeness of the evening fade.

The oven timer dinged. His meal was ready. He pushed away from the computer. Every step echoed around him as if to remind him of what he did not have.

Her words came back to him, as if following into the kitchen. *I never want to live in a world where a little boy's love is something that is best forgotten.*

He had been so wrong about Lucy. She wasn't like his biological mother, not at all. Lucy knew what mattered most in this life. She was the kind of woman who loved in a way that not even death could stop.

He didn't believe in the fairy tale of love and marriage. For the first time in his adult life he wanted to though.

* * *

Lucy would have been alarmed had she noticed the snow that fell during Katherine's shower, but she was too busy having a wonderful time. Over fifty women were squeezed into Katherine's living room, and she had the best time. Sure, there were a few of those shower games, which she always embarrassingly won, but mostly it was lots of laughing, talking and eating baked goods.

"I'll be happy to donate a holiday cake for Project Santa," Ava said. The shower was breaking up and everyone was heading out. "I'll throw in as many cookies as you want at cost."

"That's more than fair. Thank you." How fun for the kids. She would have to remember to add that to her computerized list.

"Oh, I have the best idea." Ava bounced in place in her enthusiasm. "You have to come for the McKaslin cookie bake-a-thon. We do it every Christmas."

A hand landed on Lucy's shoulder. It was Dorrie, apple-cheeked and glowing. "Wonderful idea, Ava. Yes, that's just what we should do. You must come, Lucy."

"I'm a terrible baker." She had to be honest. "I guess I'm passable if I don't forget to keep an eye on the oven."

"Then we will put you on the decoration squad." Aubrey sidled close, looking content with a hand resting on her growing abdomen. "We can ice cookies together. We'll let Dorrie and Gran bake."

"I usually bake, too," Katherine called from the corner, where she was heaped in beautiful presents on either side. "But this year, it looks like I'll be on sprinkles duty."

Sprinkles duty? Lucy couldn't believe this family. They were the kind of people she wrote about—warm and wonderful and fun. "I'm not artistic, so doing sprinkles might be safer."

"Excellent." Rebecca crowded close, her impressive engagement ring winking. "I love to put the icing ornaments on the Christmas tree cookies. Lucy, I'll show you how."

"Oh, and we make the candy cane cookies." Lauren leaned in to add. "You could help me twist them."

"Lucy should have Christmas with us, right?" Danielle pitched in.

"Yes, you must come, Lucy." Gran took hold of Lucy's arm, holding on tightly. Hope twinkled in her eyes.

"Yes, say yes, Lucy," Ava pleaded.

"As if I can say no," she said. Even if she wanted to, it would be impossible to disappoint any of these nice women. "I'm flying back to Portland the day after Christmas, but I would be honored to spend the holiday with your family."

Voices rose in happiness, but it was the cold whip of winter wind that caught Lucy's attention and the man who strode into sight, stealing a little piece of her heart. Spence.

No one else noticed him, as they were too busy talking about Christmas dinner and asking if she liked ham or turkey.

"I like everything," she assured Gran and Dorrie. "But I'm going to bring something, too. I have a great baked bean recipe that everybody seems to like."

"Perfect," Dorrie pronounced. "That's just what we need."

"Yes, baked beans." Gran looked quite pleased. "Why don't we fix the ham? That would go quite nicely together. Oh, there's Kelly. Kelly, dear, will you and that handsome husband of yours be joining us?"

Lucy heard nothing more. Over the top of his step-mother's head, Spence was grinning at her, unguarded and amused. She remembered how cozy it had felt sharing an evening at home with him. Their online chat had made her laugh and laugh. Maybe it was the two pieces of cake she'd had, but she felt brighter simply because he was near.

"I'll wait outside," he mouthed, gesturing with his thumb toward the door. He exited as quietly as he had come in.

Lucy barely remembered saying her goodbyes to the McKaslin women or the gift bag of goodies Katherine pressed into her hand as they hugged. The very pregnant Katherine glowed with excitement, and she looked well enough to be up running around. It was hard to believe she was high risk. All the prayers were helping. Lucy gently thanked her and headed toward the door.

Torrential snowfall battered her. Husbands were showing up now, lovingly arriving to pick up their wives. Ava's strapping husband was accompanied by a golden retriever that bounced happily at his side. Aubrey's quiet husband was standing beside their SUV, in conversation with Caleb and Rebecca's fiancé, Chad. Jack, the man of the house, was finishing up another pass with the snow shovel while Spence was sprinkling deicer on the walking surfaces. He didn't look up as she approached, although she caught the hint of a smile in the corners of his mouth.

He was aware of her, just as she was aware of him. Her spirit felt tingly as she went on by. She could not be falling for Spence. As wonderful as he was, he was not the kind of man she was looking for. He was too emotionally closed off. He was too harsh. He was a man who kept his loved ones at an arm length's and everyone else much farther.

But did her heart listen? No. Her heart saw all his goodness, every strength and every asset.

"Hi, Lucy." Brice, Ava's husband, nodded a greeting. "Rex, down—"

"I don't mind." Lucy laughed as the big retriever launched up and laid his front paws on her shoulders. His warm doggy tongue slapped across his cheek and loving brown eyes glowed at her adoringly. "Hi there, handsome guy."

Rex wagged his tail, gave her another dog kiss and loped through the snow in the flower beds to greet the next woman exiting the house.

It was Spence's grandmother. The big man put down his work and came to her side. Everything about him changed as he offered the frail lady his arm. He was no longer iron and granite but gentlemanly kindness.

Lucy waded into the snow toward her car, and her heart gave one big sigh. A glimpse of the real Spence McKaslin, she thought. Mystery solved.

Chapter Eleven

W̲aiting for Spence was killing her. Lucy kept looking over her shoulder every two seconds to peer down the hospital hallway. If she kept this up, she was going to get whiplash. It was merely curiosity, she told herself, not because she was sweet on the man. And it certainly *was not* because she couldn't wait to see him.

"This is a welcome contribution." Ellen, one of the floor nurses, took the first movie out of the bag Lucy had brought. She showed it to the other two nurses standing behind the counter. "There has to be a dozen Christmas movies here. Oh, the kids are going to love these."

"Good. Maybe it will help make this a more normal Christmas season for them, even if they are here." The back of her neck tingled, and she whirled around. Spence stepped out of the men's restroom wearing a Santa suit and a scowl.

"I look lame." He tugged at the furry white collar.

He looked like a dream, a big masculine man doing a favor for the kids. He looked like a Christmas wish all wrapped up in red satin. Her spirit ached with hopes she dared not give life to. Wanting him to be right for her would not make it so.

She walked toward him, digging around in the second shopping bag she had brought and pulling out two more garments. "You will feel better when you have your hat on."

"A hat?" He looked alarmed as he zeroed in on what she was carrying. "That's not a hat. It's a dunce cap with fur."

"Ebenezer, where is your Christmas spirit?"

"I left it in the truck with the Ghost of Christmas Past." He scowled harder.

He really was a funny guy. She handed him the hat. "Look, I've got one, too. You're not alone."

"How come you don't have a suit?" He yanked on the hat.

"Because I'm your helper."

A likely story. He knew he looked less than dignified. Good thing he didn't know anyone here or this would shoot holes in his hard-won reputation.

"I think you are great for doing this." She gazed up at him with gratitude in her beautiful green eyes.

He swallowed hard, wishing he were a stronger man. He had agreed to wear this dumb suit because he hadn't been able to say no to her. *If* he wanted to let feelings into his heart—not that he did—they would be as bright and as rich as the lights flashing on the Christmas tree just ahead. Good thing his heart was as unresponsive as a hard layer of winter ice.

"I'm an idiot," he told her gruffly. That was simply the truth. His brain emptied of all common sense whenever she was near. "We're finding someone else to play Santa on Christmas morning or I'm quitting. That's the way it has to be."

"Maybe a candy cane would put you in a sweeter mood." She pulled a brightly striped cane from the bag she carried.

"Sorry, lady, this is as sweet as I get."

"I don't believe that for a second, Ebenezer."

When Lucy smiled, it was as if the world stopped spinning. His world surely did. His pulse flatlined. His soul stilled. His spirit leaned toward her just a little bit. And his lips really wanted to know if her kiss was sweeter than any candy.

He scowled harder. He didn't approve of kissing. Too bad, he thought, easing back a step. Disappointment darkened Lucy's eyes. He gulped in some air, surprised. It was nice to know that if he had kissed her, she wouldn't have whacked him in the head with her shopping bag.

He deserved at least that. He had no right wanting anything meaningful with a woman like Lucy. She sparkled like the light winking off the tinsel on the Christmas tree. He was no longer falling for her. He had already fallen hard.

"Santa!" A little girl in a pair of bright pink pajamas with ballerinas printed on them and a matching robe padded out into the hallway. She had beautiful brown eyes and her round face was framed by loose black curls. "Look, Mama. Santa came."

A mother wearing the markings of deep worry and exhaustion towered protectively behind her child. "What a lovely surprise, Santa. It was nice of you to stop by when you have so much left to do up at the North Pole."

He was reminded of his sister, Danielle, who had practically lived at the hospital when Jonas had been in an unresponsive coma. It was like a nail striking deep. He looked down at the frail little girl who had grabbed

ahold of his knee. She was about his niece Madison's
age, probably three. He cleared his throat. "I've got the
elves working overtime so I could fly out here."

"Where are your reindeers?"

Other children, drawn by curiosity, walked from their
rooms into the hall. Their wonder and need to believe in
goodness was like a whisper in silence. "I left them up
on the roof. Good thing I brought Rudolph so the medi-
cal helicopter can see them if it needs to land."

"Wow." A little boy clasped his hands together. His
mother was behind him, a hand on his IV tree. "Rudolph
is my favorite. Can we see him?"

"They have a strict No Reindeer policy in this hospital. We have to follow the rules." Spence improvised
as more children gathered around him—children of all
colors and cultures and ages, adored and beloved children who were bone-thin, or missing hair or recovering
from surgery. One boy, about his nephew Tyler's age,
leaned on hand crutches, missing one leg.

Tears burned in Spence's throat as the children waved
at Lucy. The first little girl whispered, "Lucy, you know
Santa."

"That's right, Arielle. I told him about all of you.
Santa was so impressed that he had to come meet such
brave and good kids."

"Did you get my letter, Santa?" The first little boy
sidled closer. "Did ya?"

So much need in that one's eyes. On all of their faces,
he realized as he looked from one to another. Lucy's
words came back to him, compassionate and wonderful Lucy. *These children need Christmas.*

I'm not enough for this, he thought, panicking. Lucy
was watching him with quiet expectation, as if she
thought he was someone more, someone better. She

was wrong, and he hated that. The last thing he wanted to do was disappoint these kids, so he knelt down, taking time to add a little prayer. *Please Lord, a little help. Just a little.*

Then it clicked. He recognized the little boy's picture from Lucy's file folder. Good thing he had an eye for computer printouts, as they were his life. "Yes, I did receive your letter, Max. Have you been a good boy this year?"

Max nodded solemnly, scattering his brown hair. "Real good. I promise. I've been trying my very hardest."

An older woman, who was watching over Max, spoke up. She was probably his grandmother. "Max was saying he wanted a puppy, and we were hoping that you could bring one to his house on Christmas morning."

"Not a problem." Spence saw the gratitude in the grandmother's eyes and knew there would be a wiggling puppy under the tree for Max. "I'll bring you the very best one."

"Thank you, Santa. I getta go home for Christmas." Max vibrated excitedly. "*Maybe.* We hafta wait and see."

Suddenly all the kids were talking over the top of one another. Lucy took him by the hand. It was like touching heaven, like being led by a dream. She smiled up at him and hooked him, heart and soul.

"I'll pass out the candy canes in the playroom if you want to visit the kids who are bedridden first." She sounded sweet. She believed in him.

"Great," he said gruffly. "Give me some of those candy canes, and I'll check on the kids still in their rooms."

"Thank you, Santa." She radiated kindness and generosity, so beautiful and real.

"Sure, I'll wear this getup anytime for you." That's what he said but what he meant was, *I love you.*

She didn't know that as she strolled away taking kids and parents with her into the Christmas-decorated playroom. Her world hadn't changed.

His had.

Snow was still falling like a torrential rainstorm as Lucy climbed out of her car in the restaurant parking lot. Spence had angled in next to her, and as he rounded the back bumper he looked like a snowman. He was cloaked in snow. She couldn't see two feet in front of her. Darkness had set in. The only light was the faint haze from the Mr. Paco's Tacos sign.

"I really appreciate this." Spence's baritone dipped low as he held the front door for her and blocked the driving snow with his brawny form. "I'm sure you probably don't go to places like this, but I'm in the mood for Mexi-fries."

"There is no cure for what ails you like Mexi-fries." He was such a funny guy. What did he think, that she dined on caviar and pâté? She didn't even like those things. Now a Mr. Paco's deluxe burrito was right up her alley. She breezed past him into the heat of the restaurant. "You did a great job as Santa. The kids loved you."

"I think I got a rash from the beard."

His scowl didn't fool her, and he didn't have a rash. His jawline was carved perfection. She wandered up to the counter. A bored-looking teenager took her order. She always got the same thing. She was a girl who knew what she liked and stuck with it. What surprised her was the way Spence sidled up behind her and added his order to hers, while pulling out his wallet like this was a date or something.

A date? Her heart froze in mid-beat. No, don't start letting your imagination run away with you, she told herself sensibly. He's just being gentlemanly. And the fact that he was an inch away from her, leaning behind her to set a twenty on the counter was just accidental closeness. Being that close made it harder to pretend she didn't like him.

"I'll go raid the salsa bar." She slipped away, glad for an excuse. Her hands trembled as she reached for the little paper cups. She couldn't seem to separate them. She wound up with three stuck together and had to concentrate on prying them apart. When she ladled the green sauce from the tub, she spilled half of it and had to go in search of the nearest napkin dispenser to wipe it up. As she was wiping, she felt the tingles on the back of her neck again.

Spence. He was right behind her. Amusement warmed his rich baritone. "Having problems?"

"Low blood sugar." It was the only response that came to mind.

"Here, let me." He took the cups and began filling them. "No wonder. You ate three candy canes. I was counting. You had to know that was a blood sugar disaster."

"I used to be tougher when it came to sugar." In fact, it was to a lot of things, including keeping her heart safe.

"Go sit down." He sounded gruff, but kindness and caring laced his tone. "I have the drinks and a basket of tortilla chips on the table. I'll finish up here."

This is what it would be like to be taken care of by him. That thought came out of nowhere. It wasn't something she *wanted* to think. Letting herself care for him would be the worst mistake.

Or would it? With every step she took away from

Spence, her spirit remained aware of him. As she meandered down the aisle between empty booths on one side and empty tables on another, images of Spence in his Santa suit battered her. She thought of the glimpse through the open doorway where he stood at Timothy's bedside, talking earnestly with the little guy. He had sat by the tree in the playroom, carefully listening to each child, making them light up with happiness.

She had been at his side, close enough to touch, taking notes for their Christmas list. Being with him had felt *right*.

"Looks like our food is up." He set the salsa on the table. "I'll be back."

Yes, being with Spence definitely felt right. She settled into the booth, watching him stride away. The spark in her soul grew painfully, taking over where her reason would not. Tenderness winked to life within her, and she tried to fight it.

There were two other couples in the restaurant. They were on the other side of the dining room, each couple speaking low in rapt conversation. She felt like that, as if her entire being were reaching toward Spence. She nibbled on a chip, wishing she could put brakes on her heart.

This cannot be love, she told herself. It can't be.

"You look pretty serious." He slid the tray on the table and eased onto the seat across from her. "How are you feeling?"

"No idea." That was only the truth. If she could go back and know only the terse, stoic, grumpy abominable snowman she always thought he was, then she would not be under the effects of his dimpled smile. She wouldn't be losing her heart.

"Here." He ripped the paper from a straw, leaving the

top inch or so on, and stabbed it into her drink. He lifted it over to her side of the table, along with her order of Mexi-fries. "Do you want to say the blessing?"

"Yes." She had a lot to be thankful for. She had a lot to think about. "Dear Father, Thank You for this meal and for the fellowship we have shared today. Please watch over the children with special love and care."

And please show me what I should do about this man I'm with, Lord, she added silently. "Amen."

"Amen." He was watching her between narrowed eyes, as if he were particularly assessing her.

What was he thinking? What were the chances he could figure out how she was feeling? She popped a Mexi-fry into the hot salsa and into her mouth. Greasy and mealy and spicy—just what a confused girl needed. She felt a little better so she helped herself to another one.

"I didn't realize you spent so much time at the hospital." He slid her burrito plate toward her along with the napkins and a plastic knife and fork. "I learned from a few of the parents that you're a regular there. You run errands for them, make calls for them, make sure they have what they need so they can spend more time with their kids."

"Yes, I do that for the critically ill children." She situated the plate in front of her, getting it just right so she didn't have to look at Spence. If there was caring on his face or kindness making his eyes deeply blue, then she was going to fall in love with him, bam, just like that, and there would be no way to stop it…no way for reason to reign.

She smoothed open one of the napkins and laid it in her lap. "I go three times a week. I do whatever is most needed. Sometimes it's reading a story to a child so the parents can run to their room and shower and change, or bring sandwiches and coffee or just listen and pray. I know how desperate and on edge parents can feel. Nothing matters but their child."

"We've had a taste of that in our family when Jonas was wounded." His baritone dipped intimately, full of honesty. "It was hard on the munchkins. Madison was too little to understand, but Tyler knew. They were away from us for the holidays, living in a hotel and seeing Jonas when they could. It's a good thing you do, Lucy. You make a difference."

"Not such a big difference." She cut into her burrito. "I wasn't the one who was Santa Claus. You brought a lot of joy to some little people who really deserved it."

"It was a sacrifice to my dignity wearing that hat." He unwrapped his first taco, fighting not to reveal the truth in his heart. "I see what you must have gone through, Lucy. My dignity is nothing when compared to that."

"Don't start being nice to me, please." She smiled but kept her focus on the swipe of her knife and fork cutting the burrito in little bites. She probably thought she was hiding her pain, but he could see it.

"Why? You're afraid you're going to start liking me more? I'm nicer than you think, Lucy."

She didn't say anything, cutting away. She was going to run out of burrito, but he understood what she couldn't say. He could see how she had been like those mothers in the children's wing, attentive and devoted, frazzled and worn and fighting not to let it show. "How could he have let you go?"

Pain creased her forehead, creating cute little lines—lines he wanted to rub away with the pads of his fingers. He fought the urge to reach across the table. The overwhelming need gripped him to right things for her. He wanted to make sure she never hurt like that again.

"When Jim lost his son, he lost his heart, too. There was simply nothing left. I did everything I could, but in the end he had closed off too much of his heart. He stopped being able to love. He didn't want me. There was nothing I could do."

She was the tragedy of it. He could see without words what had happened, maybe because he closed down his feelings, too, when he had to. It was his way of dealing.

"It had to kill a part of you to know you couldn't do anything for him." He could see that, too. "How long did you wait for him?"

"Ten years." Lucy stabbed a piece of burrito with her fork but left both fork and food on the plate. She reached for her straw and took off the bit of paper. "For the first few years after Christian's death, I stood by Jim even when he pushed me away. And he was harsh. He was hurting. I was hurting, too. I knew that if I hung in there, the Jim I knew and loved would come back to me. That was the first book I sold. I set the story in 1865 Montana, but it was a story about a man who came home from the Civil War changed and the woman who loved and waited patiently for his soul to return."

The secret to Lucy having been revealed, he set down his taco. "Her story ended happily, but yours didn't."

"True." She took a sip of iced tea, more beautiful for all that he knew about her. "Jim never returned to me. I think it was safer for him."

Safer. Wasn't that the word he often used? He reached for his tea, giving him time to think. Safe was simply being smart. Safe was prudent and wise and cautious. It's better to be safe than sideswiped by a broken vow or love falling apart.

"That's why you write?" he asked.

"It's my way to dream." She took another sip of tea. "How about you, Spence?"

"I don't approve of dreams."

"I could have guessed that." She rolled her eyes, and he loved the way she did it. She was adorable. "I meant, I've told you mine, now it's your turn to tell me about your hurt."

The air wheezed out of his lungs. "Are you sure we can't keep talking about yours?"

"Have mercy on me."

How could he refuse? He felt helpless to do anything but what she wanted. It was a definite warning sign, but he didn't seem alarmed. He ought to be, but he was sliding deeper into love with her every moment. He picked up his taco and took a bite. "I don't have any romantic tragedies to share with you."

"That's because you have never let anyone get that close to you." She pushed a stray curl out of her eyes. "Do I dare mention something must be wrong with a man your age who has never had a serious relationship?"

"Sure, go ahead and say it. Everyone else has." He took another bite. "I'm disagreeable enough that no decent woman will have me, which basically means I don't want the kind of woman who would be interested in me."

"You are impossible."

"I've heard that before." He dragged a Mexi-fry through the salsa. "I don't know how it happened. I had a few less than serious girlfriends when I was younger—"

"Less than serious?"

"I was the one who wasn't serious."

"Ah, so you were that kind of man. You never were going to love those poor girls. Not really."

"Yes, but I didn't know that. I thought—" It was his turn to roll his eyes. "I don't know what I thought. Dad had been able to make his second marriage work. Dorrie is great. I know there are decent women out there. I just panicked. Just because someone says they love you doesn't mean it's true. Or that it will turn out to be true."

"I know that for sure." She was pure understanding. "It happened to me. Love is a perilous journey."

"Which is why I've never set foot on that path."

"What happened to your mother?" She took a bite of her burrito, watching him carefully as if she thought she could figure out his truths.

This meant it was a good idea to shield his heart a little more. "Linda took off when I was thirteen. She took off in the family car with Lauren, who was about two at the time."

"She didn't just abandon you, she tore your family apart."

"That she did." Spence tried to shield away the memories of the adolescent boy who had been crushed. Linda had been one to share her unhappiness. He remembered that unhappiness now, still aching after all these years. *You ruined my life, Spencer, not just my figure. With you, it was one selfish demand after another.* "Linda forever broke my belief in happily ever afters. They are not as common as you might think."

"True, but they aren't unheard of either. Your family is full of them. Look at your sisters."

"I try not to." He didn't know how to explain that he feared even a good marriage was simply doom waiting to happen. "My sisters defy logic."

"You really are a glass-is-half-empty kind of man."

"I try to be." It was safe. It was smart, which was why he was busy sectioning off his softer emotions, the ones he had no right feeling for Lucy. This was all happening way too fast. He could not be carried away by the fairy tale of love.

And he was panicking just a little. But when he gazed at sweet Lucy, he wanted more than anything to open his heart and let her in.

Chapter Twelve

"Oh no. Look at my car." Lucy waded into the parking lot in the knee-deep snow. "What is with the weather this winter? We had maybe six inches of snow last year."

"That was an usually warm winter. This is Montana. We used to get snow like this all the time when I was a kid." He hiked through the accumulation as if it were nothing.

Sure, because he had longer legs, the snow wasn't proportionally as deep. "I can't drive in this. Look. Snow is up to the car door. Half the tires are buried."

"You are the city slicker who thought it would be a good idea to relocate here, right?" He beeped his truck remote and the locks popped. "See why I think your car is ridiculous?"

"What's wrong with my car?"

"It high centers on speed bumps." He opened his truck's passenger door, presumably for her. "Notice how my truck doesn't? I can drive home in a snowstorm."

"All I have to do is get out of the parking lot. The street is plowed. I can see the snow berm from here."

She unlocked her door and tossed her purse onto the seat. "Where did I put my ice scraper?"

"Pop the trunk." Spence closed the door and walked to the back of her car, waiting as she hit the lever. "I put it there when I dug out your car."

"I don't think you should have to scrape my windshield since you paid for dinner."

"As long as we don't make this a habit, I'll be fine with clearing off your car tonight." He started scraping her back window. "Go ahead and start up the engine. Let it get warm."

No wonder your sisters love you so much, she thought as she complied. The engine turned over, icy air blew out of the vents and she adjusted the settings. Two feet had to have fallen while they had been eating. How long had they been talking? She checked the clock in the dash. Two and a half hours! It was nearly eight o'clock.

No, that couldn't be right. Could it? She pulled out her cell phone and checked the screen. Yikes. Time had evaporated. Then again, she had been having fun talking with Spence. The trip to the hospital seemed to have opened him up. Maybe it was the power of the Christmas season or perhaps she had been wrong about Spence all along. He might be very effective at putting up walls, but he had let them down for her tonight.

Interesting. She watched the man in her rearview mirror, working at sweeping the snow off the car roof. His face was set with grim determination, but he had the spirit of a generous and giving man. Maybe it would be all right to let herself fall in love with him—just a tiny bit.

It wasn't as if she could sit around and let him do all the work. She felt under her seat for something that might work like an ice scraper. There was no telling what she might come up with. Her car wasn't messy, but things did tend to slip beneath the seat when she wasn't paying attention.

She stretched as far as she could reach and bumped something straight-edged with her fingertips. She seized it and gave a good yank. How about that—a Tupperware lid. That should work.

"What do you think you're doing?" He demanded the instant she stepped out of the car. He was working on the driver's side windows.

"I'm helping."

"With a food container lid?"

"Why not? I might as well make myself useful." She shivered as the wind gusted and drove right through her goose down coat. "Besides, it's my car."

"I don't care. You're not standing around getting chilled. This will only take a minute." He stole the lid from her gloved hands, as if he thought he were the boss of her.

Should she be indignant? It felt as if he had crossed a line. She swiped snow out of her face and gazed up at the towering man who glared down at her with unmistakable affection.

"You are too important to the Christmas project," he said softly and set her lid on the top of the roof beneath the ice scraper.

"Me? If you catch a cold, then we are out a Santa. The kids would be terribly disappointed."

"There's no replacing you, Lucy." He shook the snow off his leather gloves and cradled her chin in both hands. "You are one of a kind."

Why did he have to be like this? He made it impossible to resist falling. Love seeped into the broken places within her, wiping out a decade of loneliness and loss.

Love for him glowed like new life within her, and as they both hesitated, her pulse beat with fear.

He was going to kiss her. They both knew it. She watched his gaze settle on her mouth before his lips slanted over hers. Ever so slowly, his lips met hers in a sweet, soul-tingling kiss. She curled her fingers into the fabric of his coat, holding on. It could have been the battering push of the ruthless wind that had her losing her balance, but the truth was harder to face.

Spence ended the kiss and did not move away. He gazed down at her, letting her know that he meant what she had felt. He also was debating about kissing her again.

Panic lashed at her, and she held on to him tightly. As long as she didn't move, then she wouldn't have the urge to leap into her car and race off, despite the depth of the snow and her uncleared windshield. It was scary thinking about taking a step onto a romantic path. The last time she loved a man, he had left her devastated.

"Please get into the car where it's warm so I can finish up the windows." He handed her the lid. "Let me do this for you."

His tenderness melted her fear. She complied, but only because she was in love with him—completely, foolishly, one hundred percent in love.

He was just about done with women he had to worry about, Spence thought as he shoveled the walkway. Why did he have to go and kiss Lucy? Now there was another woman he was worried over. He leaned the shovel against the hedge, pulled his coat cuff back and angled his watch toward the porch light. Nine minutes after nine. Lucy should have called by now to tell him she was safely home.

He thought of the roads out in her direction. Fear nibbled at his gut. He should have put his foot down and made her stay in town. Anything could have happened out there on those roads—a slide off, a fallen tree or power lines, wildlife in the roadway. And that was all if the county had managed to plow the road. Her little car was going to high center and then she would be stuck. He did his best not to imagine other vehicles slamming into her and all sorts of injury and horrible outcomes.

If his momentary lapse of judgment in kissing her wasn't proof enough, then this was. He only worried about people he loved. Love could do him in, render him vulnerable in a way there could never be any protection against.

He grabbed the shovel, mad at himself. He didn't want to be in love with Lucy. He stomped down the walkway, which was already accumulating more snow, and grumbled all the way into the garage. His truck stood like a silent reminder of all he had done tonight. He had shoveled Lucy's car out of the deep accumulation, drove a path for her the short distance to the main road and then cut down the central lane between the tires with the shovel he had borrowed from the restaurant. That way she could make it onto the plowed road.

Oh, he was in love with her, about as in love as a man like him could get. He tossed the shovel against the wall and hit the button. As the door cranked down, he kicked the snow off his boots, wishing he hadn't kissed her tonight. Then he wouldn't be tied up in knots wondering what could have happened to her. It wasn't smart to care this much.

He kicked off his boots and marched into the kitchen, shedding his gloves and coat as he went. He hung them to dry over the kitchen chairs and bumped up the ther-

mostat. Another minute had passed and there was still
no call.

I'm calling her, he decided. He couldn't take waiting. He was an impatient man—or, at least that's what
he told himself. Fear stuck in his stomach. He had to
know she was okay.

The phone rang in his hand. Lucy's name and number flashed on the screen. He punched the answer key.
"Yep?"

"Spence, it's me. I'm home safe and sound."

Whew. Talk about relief. The starch went out of his
knees, and he put a hand on the edge of the counter.
"Good. How were the roads?"

"The plow was in front of me, so I followed it until I
hit my driveway. My car got stuck about two feet in so
I had to walk, but I'm here. Bean was glad to see me.
Her bowl was halfway down."

"Tragedy adverted."

"Exactly. She says hi, by the way. I think she's a
teeny bit fond of you."

"I can say the same about her." He wasn't talking
about the cat, but it was the best he could do at saying what he meant. She was safe. She was an adequate
driver. Why wouldn't she be safe? But it wasn't logic
that had him worrying over her. It was love—undeni-
able, unstoppable love.

"I want to thank you again, Spence. I had a surpris-
ingly nice time."

"Glad to hear it. I'm sure it was the Mexi-fries, not
the company."

"Oh, I don't know about that. It's not every girl who
can say she had dinner with Santa Claus."

"I can say the same thing about sharing tortilla chips
with Santa's helper." She charmed him when no other

woman had been able to get close. Why? He paced down the hallway, turning on lights on his way to the living room. "Speaking of which, I'm assuming you got down what every kid wanted from Santa?"

"I did. Tomorrow I'll start contacting parents and working out the details. A few siblings were visiting so I was able to get them in my list, but we don't want to leave anyone out."

"I'll have one of my employees go through the store and pick out anything on your list, if that will help."

"I know it's your busy time of year, and I'd hate to bother one of your employees. Why don't I do that after hours?"

"Sure. I won't even hide in my office. How's that for having the Christmas spirit?"

"A definite improvement." She chuckled, rich and low.

The feelings rolled through him, making it impossible to keep a tight rein on his heart. He was walking on dangerous ground, but did it stop him? No. He had never wanted anything as much as the chance to see Lucy again and to simply be alone with her taking in her smile, her laugh and her sweetness.

"What about the rest of the shopping?" he asked. "Christmas is getting closer."

"Yikes. I know. We're running out of shopping days fast. I was going to sort through my list tonight and split it up. I had planned to have our volunteers do at least half of the shopping. Why shouldn't they have fun, too?"

He expected as much. He hit the switch for the gas fireplace and dropped into his recliner. He felt relaxed and content. "Why don't you and I take the other half?"

"Do you have time?"

"In the evenings, sure." He had a crammed full schedule, but none of that was stressing him out.

"It sounds perfect. I have a lot of work this week, too. I also have the McKaslin bake-a-thon on Wednesday night."

"Then we had better make the most of our free time this week. Give me a call after church tomorrow, and we'll figure out where to meet."

"Sounds good to me. Hey, Spence?"

Uh-oh. He recognized that tone. "What?"

"I'm glad to see you caught a little bit of Christmas cheer. It looks good on you. Well, good night."

"'Night."

He hated that she was hanging up. It was late and getting later. Saying goodbye was the sensible thing. But he wanted to talk with her some more…hear how she grew up…amusing family stories…that kind of thing.

He sat staring into the dancing flames for a long while, thinking over the day with Lucy. It was funny how thinking of her made the house feel less lonely and his life less empty.

If only she could get their kiss out of her mind. Lucy scowled in frustration as she pulled her car to a stop in the plowed lot. It was Sunday afternoon, and the bookstore was closed. She was the lone car on this side of the lot. The rest of the shopping center, newly renovated, was bursting with shoppers. Folks walked to and from stores, loaded down with their purchases.

You can't sit here and watch them forever. She huffed out a breath and took her key from the ignition. Although sitting in a cold car forever would be easier than facing the man who had kissed her with such tenderness, she could not stop dreaming of it. It was scary trusting someone with her heart again, but what was the alternative?

A shadow moved in the store. Spence was striding her way. He wore a black long-sleeve T-shirt and jeans. He unlocked the front door and poked his head out. He certainly looked glad to see her.

That was how she felt, too, brimming with happiness from simply seeing him. She grabbed her purse and was hardly aware of how she got to the door, only that she was with him.

"Thanks for coming this late." He waited until she stepped inside to lock the door after her. "I want to leave the lights on low, if you don't mind. I don't want one of my sisters driving by and noticing the two of us here together. The next thing you know, my phone will be ringing off the hook."

"I understand." She felt the same way. What was happening between them was private. There was nothing more personal than matters of the heart. She slipped out of her coat. "I caught sight of you in church, but you were with your grandmother so I didn't intrude. Did you get her home all right?"

"Sure did." He took her coat and slung it over the back of a chair. "I worry about her in this weather. It wouldn't take much for her to slip in the ice and break a hip. I shoveled and deiced her walkways, but more snow is forecast for tonight."

"You take good care of your family." This was one of the things she loved about him.

"Family is the most important thing on this earth." His voice rang with sincerity.

He had always been deeply committed to those he loved, always faithful and serving. Nothing could be more attractive in a good man. She swooned, just a little, praying he didn't notice. "I agree. I'm deeply-committed to everyone I love."

"We're more alike than I ever would have thought."

She pulled the list out of her pocket. "We both like Mexi-fries. I never would have pegged you for a Mexi-fry eater."

"I can be surprising. When I first met you, I couldn't have guessed you devoted a lot of your time to helping others."

"I can't believe you remember meeting me. It was near inventory or something and you hardly looked at me. You couldn't have noticed me enough to even have an impression."

"It was May. The sun was shining. You were wearing a yellow dress, and you had your hair down and curly." He held out his hand for the list.

"You remember all that?"

"Yep. It would be hard not to. You and Katherine hit it off, and that's when she started bugging me about asking you out." He took the printout from her and winced. What he should have said was *I remember because when you walked into the store, it was like the sun shining for the first time.*

But saying that was personal. It would be opening himself up. He didn't like being vulnerable. He was no good at it.

Lucy, not knowing how he felt, smiled in that light, easy way of hers. "I had no idea about the bugging. No wonder you scowled so hard at me every time you saw me and invested your energy in avoiding me."

"Katherine was determined. All my sisters are." He glanced at the list, organized by section and title. He loved a woman who knew how to sensibly organize. "Don't worry about the bugging. I'm immune to it."

"Then why did you avoid me?" She walked after him into the stacks. "I mean, if you were truly immune, then whatever they said wouldn't have bothered you, and you could have at least said hello to me once in a while."

"I said I was immune to them, not to you." He choked. He had gone *way* too far. He never meant to be so honest. It might be a good idea to close up a little and frown to compensate.

"I noticed you, too," she said, showing all honesty. She had never looked so lovely, her eyes luminescent, her heart showing. "I remember thinking you looked like a really great man."

"You did?" Why that shocked him, he couldn't say. "I wasn't nice to you."

"Which is why I stopped thinking that. But now that I know you—" She didn't finish, but she did blush.

What she didn't say lingered between them, unspoken and yet somehow felt. Tenderness ebbed into him like Christmas cheer. He was a fool, he knew it, but it looked like Lucy really liked him. Why she liked him remained a mystery, but he wasn't going to panic. Yet. Like was a long way from love. He didn't expect her to love him, not a woman as shining and true as Lucy. That meant there were no expectations, no fears about how impossible it would be for love to last.

When he gazed down at her, the tender affection within him doubled. He didn't want it to. He couldn't seem to stop it. Lost in the moment, he longed for her sweetness. She was a balm to his loneliness and hurt. She made the darkness and the shadows fade.

She made his defenses weak, and he slanted his mouth over hers. He watched her eyes widen with surprise and then go dreamy. Maybe those were his secret dreams he saw in those emerald depths, not hers.

He wasn't a man who approved of dreams and there they were, silent and waiting, for him to grab hold and claim them.

He was too smart to believe in dreams, but he kissed her anyway. Or maybe he was not that strong. Either way, commitment seized him with an iron grip, leaving him committed to this fragile sunshine of a woman who could never be his.

Chapter Thirteen

Now she couldn't get their two kisses out of her mind. Lucy sighed and checked her half of the list. The computer printout blurred. She blinked twice and still couldn't bring the letters into focus. Impossible. All she could see was Spence at the other end of the aisle, slipping books out of their places and into the basket he held.

His powerful shoulders were set straight, his movements sure, his presence commanding. Being on the project had changed him, and those changes looked very good on him. Love shimmered inside her like light on Christmas tinsel. She had been wrong about him. She had thought he was closed off and harsh, but now she could see beneath the mask he presented to the world. She saw a much different man, a kind, amazing, strong man who never let anyone down.

Surely he would not let her down.

"How's it coming down there?" He broke the silence between them.

"I'm almost done with my list."

"I'm done." He strolled her way, his basket brimming with books. "Where do you want to put all this?"

"Last year the committee chair volunteered her house for storage."

"Then I'll take this home with me, since I'm here in town. A huge snowstorm could blow in and trap all the presents at your house."

"Good idea. More snow is in the forecast."

"I can spare a few employees to help with the wrapping."

"The more the merrier."

"Glad we got that all squared away." He took the heavy basket from her, their fingers brushing. Gentleness crept through him. "Are you ready to hit the toy store?"

"I'm ready for anything."

She obviously hadn't spent much time in the toy store during the height of the shopping season. He hiked toward his office. "I'll be right back."

It was nice to know that it was no longer just his eyes that malfunctioned around her, because now he had a whole new set of problems. Just like his eyes searching to keep sight of her, his ears strained for the familiar sounds of her gait on the carpet and the rustle of her movements. His brain kept going over how her face had changed after their kiss, how soft and vulnerable she had looked. That kiss had changed him, too.

Not that he wanted to think about that, though.

He stored the baskets in the corner, next to two others that were equally as full. He grabbed his coat and gloves. The store had always contributed for Christmas charity programs, but this year doing more felt right. He couldn't remember the last time he had been this satisfied and content, and Lucy had nothing to do with that.

Or at least that's what he told himself. That's what he had to cling to.

He was aware of every step that brought him closer to her. She stood near the front door in her coat ready to go. He felt big towering over her. She was small and dainty, and his soul hurt with a strange intensity. He feared he knew why, and he did not want to cope with that either.

"Should we both drive over separately?" she asked.

"Why don't you ride shotgun with me? I wouldn't mind the company."

"I wouldn't mind either." The way she smiled up at him made his chest seize up tight.

Panic drummed through him. What did he think he was doing? As he led the way toward the back door, where his truck was parked, he knew he was two thousand times a fool. He didn't believe in love. He thought of Dad and Dorrie. Okay, he didn't want to believe in love. He didn't want to be blinded, because that's what love did to a man.

Already it was happening. All he could see was Lucy's beauty and charm, her vulnerability, her loving nature and nothing else. She was like a Christmas tree on Christmas morning, so lovely and breathtaking that it overpowered every shadow.

He had to remember this wasn't real. Love could be an illusion. How was a man to tell the difference?

"It must be meaningful to be a part of a family legacy like this." Lucy broke into his thoughts. "You must have grown up in this bookstore. You must have walked down these decorated aisles every year since you were a toddler."

"I saw that smirk. You're trying to imagine me as a toddler."

"I've got a pretty good imagination, but even I can't picture that."

He liked the warmth in her voice, the melody of her tone, the way when she spoke, his spirit leaned toward her, as if yearning to hear more. "I was a pretty serious toddler."

"I believe that."

"I wasn't the happiest little kid on the planet." He shrugged away the memory and armed the security panel by the back door. Punching in numbers helped him to gloss over those hard times. "My mom wasn't so good with toddlers."

"Why did she have so many children?"

"She liked babies." He held the back door for her. Cold air whipped at them.

"Babies but not toddlers. Not children?"

His throat tightened, and he couldn't answer. He checked the lock so she couldn't see his face. How could he tell her the truth? It was him his mother hadn't liked.

"I'm glad you have Dorrie." Lucy's gloved hand settled on his.

Emotion threatened to roll over him. He set his shoulders, determined to keep it back. "She seems to tolerate me okay."

"I tolerate you okay, too," she said.

It sounded an awful lot like love in her tone, an awful lot like that emotion he could not trust. He put his head down, determined not to let it affect him or panic him. He twined his fingers between hers, locking their hands together.

"I hope you're up for this, because I'm not." He wasn't talking about facing the jam-packed toy store.

"I am not afraid because I have you, Spence. You

are a big solid man. You can bulldoze your way down the aisles."

She could tease a smile out of him and make his fear ebb. With her smaller hand tucked safely in his, they waded through the snow together.

Lucy stood on her tiptoes and stretched as high as she could, but her fingertips could only bump the top shelf and not the box she was reaching for.

"I'll get it." Spence came up behind her. His nearness was dizzying as he handily hefted the boxed doll from the shelf. He took a step back, putting space between them. He was smiling, but his eyes were serious as he slid the present into one of their four carts. "See? I'm good for something."

"I'm keeping track." She winked at him. "Pushing carts, plowing through crowds and getting stuff off the top shelf."

"You forgot my mathematical abilities. We still have three hundred forty-two dollars and six cents left on our budget."

"You're a walking calculator. You know what this means?"

"I'm afraid to ask."

"I'm going to recommend you stay on the committee."

"You think I'm going to do this again next year?" He shook his head and tossed her the grinch look. "I have a headache from all this noise. And what is that sound? There should be a law against toys that make so much noise."

Some kid in the next aisle over was playing with something that made a piercing siren sound. Only an air-raid siren would be quieter.

She would have believed Spence's scowl, but she knew him now. The scowl was all for show. She didn't let it bother her.

"What's next?" she asked instead, since he had commandeered the toy list.

"The doll clothes are the next aisle over. That way—" He nodded to their left, away from the siren sound, and grabbed two of the loaded carts, leaving her the empty ones to push. "I'm not sure, but I think the doll cradles are in that aisle, too."

She bit her lip.

"I saw that. You're laughing at me." He scowled harder, pulling the cart filled with dolls. "I have a niece."

"And you have shopped here for her more than once or twice."

"It's an uncle's job. I have to buy her a lot of stuff. I'm no slacker."

"I understand. You have a reputation to protect."

"Exactly." He turned the corner, avoided more doll accessory shoppers and halted in front of the cradles. He pointed mid-aisle. "The doll clothes are there."

"I'll do the clothes." She leaned close to get a good look at the list. Moving closer to him made those wishes shoot like stars to the surface.

"Go ahead and take the list." He handed it to her. "I only have two things to pick out."

She bit her lip, watching Spence pick out cradles for some of the dolls in his cart. For the first time in over a decade, she could see her dreams with life and color: Spence picking out Christmas gifts for their little girl—

Stop that thought right there. She squeezed her eyes shut briefly, willing the image away. When she opened her eyes, she focused on the racks of packaged doll clothes in front of her. She had to concentrate on what was real.

"Looks like you need help." A few minutes later, Spence was at her side.

"You have opinions on doll fashions?"

"Madison has excellent fashion sense, and she has trained me well." Spence did not even blush.

Her heart tumbled a little more in love with him. He would make a great dad. "I would appreciate your expertise."

"Madison would go for pink or purple. And sparkles over plain." He checked the list, leaning close enough that his cheek rested against her temple.

Everything within her calmed. It was like being wrapped in peace.

"Definitely go with the sparkles." He was talking about the clothes, but all she could hear was the whispers of her dreams. Spending every day with him. Grocery shopping and book shopping and toy shopping. Cooking dinner, sharing Mexi-fries and nachos, and riding in his truck. Sharing everyday things and extraordinary moments and memories just like this.

"I'll go with the pink dresses and the sparkly shoes."

"Excellent choice. Madison would approve." He moved away, but it didn't feel as if any space separated them.

She felt closer to him as she chose the packages. He took the plastic containers from her and dumped them into one of his carts.

"Toy horses are next," she said, hardly aware of reading the list, no longer aware of the piercing siren or the noisy store or the shoppers pushing in.

"Follow me." He led the way down the aisle like a conquering hero.

Her heart was full. "Have you ever noticed how bossy you are?"

"I haven't noticed it, no." He flashed his dimples at her. "But I've heard that complaint before."

"I can't imagine why."

"I told you. I have more than a few flaws." He was forced to stop in the main aisle due to a traffic jam. Carts were pointed every which way. Kids milled underfoot. Parents had dazed looks. "I'm suddenly reminded of Christmas shopping when I was little."

"You were like that family right there." She gestured toward parents with four children, two girls and two boys, wide-eyed with excitement. "You were just like that older brother, trying to keep his siblings in line."

"It's a tough job. I have nothing but respect for that kid. I know his woes."

"I've met your family. I'm sure the woes were huge."

"There was Katherine, who was always perfect. I could count on her to be sensible, but then there was Ava." He scowled, but he wasn't scowling inside. "She was very unreliable. See that little girl trying to hang upside down from the shopping cart? That was Ava. I barely survived her toddlerhood."

"You worry over her. You still do."

"Sure she's married and expecting, but what if she has a daughter just like her? I'll be a bundle of nerves again."

"You have an overdeveloped sense of responsibility."

"That sounds about as desirable as being exposed to the bubonic plague." The question was, would a dreamer of a woman think that was a good thing? He couldn't see it. "What were your Christmases like growing up?"

"Stockings on the hearth and Christmas cookies to nibble on. It was a secular holiday in my family, but there was always an angel on the top of our tree and lots of family time. My dad would play Christmas songs on our piano."

"Do you play?"

"Badly. I stopped torturing the poor instrument long ago."

She was being modest, he was sure of it. He couldn't imagine Lucy doing anything poorly. The carts ahead of him began to move, and he inched forward. "Our Christmases were homier after Dorrie came. She was good at all those touches: garlands on the mantel, a wreath on the door. You already know about the Christmas cookie baking session every year."

"And I'm looking forward to it. I've invested in a wide variety of sprinkles to add to the cookie decoration choices. It sounds as if we both had typical American Christmases."

"Family-centered. Faith-centered." Remembering warmed the places in his heart, which had been cold for so long. "Every year Gran and Grandpop would crowd us into the back of their car and take us to the candlelight ceremony. It was my favorite."

"Mine, too."

"It's time to remember a night two thousand years ago and be thankful to Him." That was a little too personal for him, so he changed the subject. "Our Christmases have changed. Next year, there are going to be more nieces and nephews."

"Everyone is breaking off into family units."

"That's the way it's meant to be." What he didn't say was the obvious—how his future looked to be the same stretch of responsibility and loneliness. He didn't know how to change it.

"Katherine is due on Thursday. Surely the baby will be here for Christmas."

"He'll be the second Christmas baby in the family. Madison missed Christmas by a day. Danielle went into labor right as Dorrie was setting the Christmas ham on the table. Gran stayed behind with Tyler and made to-go plates. She sent Dad with them and the presents. We celebrated in the cafeteria, eating and unwrapping. It was an event."

"I've been praying for Katherine and her baby. Her being high risk has to be a big worry for all of you."

"Huge, but she's doing great so far." His chest seized up every time he thought of it. "I have to go through this with three more sisters this coming year."

"Your scowl isn't fooling me. You're worried, not annoyed."

"How did you know?" She was getting very good at figuring him out.

"I'm not revealing my sources. You are not as mysterious as you think."

What else had she figured out? Could she see other things about him, namely his affection for her? He looked down one aisle and dragged the carts along.

"Could you reach that box down for me?" Lucy was up on her tiptoes again, looking adorable wearing a red Christmas sweater with a huge yarn Christmas tree on it. She was wholesome and dear and Christmassy, everything he wanted to believe in, everything he wanted to trust.

"No problem." He reached behind her to snag the box off the top shelf. Silken strands of her golden hair brushed against his jaw. He was so near to her he could feel his spirit long for hers like the night waited for morning.

Love, impossibly deep and infinitely committed, hammered through him like redemption. All he had to do was let down the walls around his heart, let the emotion sweep through him and fill his soul. There would be no more loneliness, no more long empty evenings and weekends.

If he let Lucy into his heart, he would be needed. He would be loved. He would have every dream he had ever wanted to dream. *Maybe.* Panic punched him with an adrenaline rush.

He stepped away and put the box in one of the carts.

"Great. Thanks." She bent over the list, her hair tumbling over her shoulders. "Truck aisle, here we come."

"I have some expertise in that field thanks to Tyler."

"You are more Santa than Scrooge, Spence McKaslin." When she gazed at him with approval like that, her affection was plain to see.

Affection, sure, but how much? What if she did come to love him? Then what? Panic kicked up a notch. He couldn't see her loving him truly to the depths of the soul, to the ends of the earth and beyond life. Not him. He felt ready to break apart. It was too much strain on his cardiovascular system. His heart hurt in ways he could not measure.

"Lucy? Is that you?" A woman's voice broke above the store's noise.

He glanced over his shoulder at a middle-aged woman with round glasses and a friendly smile, who was heading directly toward them with a loaded-down cart.

Lucy glanced up from her list. "Carol, how good to see you again. How have you been?"

"Fine, dear. Busy, but fine." The woman—Carol— wove around her cart to give Lucy a brief hug. That didn't surprise him. Everyone loved Lucy. Even a grinch like him.

"Carol Roberts, this is Spence McKaslin." Lucy sidled up to him as if she wasn't afraid to introduce him to her friends at all. "Carol's little girl was in the hospital this time last year. Bethany is still doing well?"

"Very well." Carol's bright smile left no doubt. "It's good to meet you, Mr. McKaslin."

"Good to meet you." He nodded grimly, fearing the woman was wondering what he was doing with a ray of sunshine like Lucy.

"We're shopping for Project Santa." Lucy explained, gesturing to their carts.

"You have no idea how wonderful it was last Christmas. Between the generosity and the cheer, Santa Claus and your pastor, we found the strength and hope to get Bethany through cancer treatment." Tears stood in the woman's eyes. "I'll keep you all in my prayers this Christmas so that other children will be as fortunate as my little girl."

Spence took a step away from Lucy. He thought of the children he had met in the hospital. He prayed they would find happy resolutions, too. He saw Lucy in a different light as she gave Mrs. Roberts another hug and they made promises to get together for lunch after the new year.

She was loved by everyone. She might not talk about it or even realize it, but it was true. Not only did she make a difference with her volunteer work but she made lasting friendships as well. People, including his family, adored her, and why wouldn't they? She was kind and loving and lovable.

He had driven everyone else away but his family,

and he couldn't even show them—the people he trusted most—love.

"It was nice to meet you, Mr. McKaslin." Mrs. Roberts smiled and took off with her cart, having already said goodbye to Lucy.

"I have been meaning to call her." Lucy checked the list. "It was divine intervention. A sign."

Yes, that was what he was thinking, too. He did his best to manage what he hoped was something resembling a smile as he reversed the carts and navigated into the busy main aisle. He was distracted by the sinking sensation of his heart returning to its rightful place.

When he glanced over his shoulder, she was right behind him, looking full of joy and love and life. She made him love her; she made him need her. She made him want to dream. He, the man who did not believe in dreams, wanted to wish on the first star tonight and see his future with Lucy in it.

"Do you have a headache from all the noise?" she asked. "I do. Ava's bakery is open tonight. When we're done with all our shopping, I'm going to stop by and get something chocolate. Want to come with me?"

Her smile nearly suffocated him because he did not want to face the truth. He loved her, how he loved her with every bit of his heart and every piece of his soul. He did not want to think about the future beyond tonight. It was pointless.

"I could use some chocolate," he said, when he should have been saying no.

He wasn't strong enough to open up to her. He didn't know how, so he stayed quiet. The truth remained like a cold chunk of ice in his heart—his miserly heart. Dorrie was right. Danielle was right. They were all right.

He wasn't the man for Lucy, no matter how much he wanted to be. He didn't have enough heart to give her the great love she deserved.

Chapter Fourteen

"Hi, Spence." His cousin, Brianna, smiled up at him from behind the cash register in Ava's shop. "This must be Lucy. Oh, it's so nice to meet you. Ava's talked a lot about you."

He scowled. This had been the entire evening. The cashier at the toy store. A woman in the mall parking lot. The clerk stocking magazines at the mall bookstore. A little boy standing in line for the center court Santa Claus. Everyone adored her. They hugged her, told him how wonderful she was and all the nice things she had done—sat by a widow's side during her son's surgery, found a place to stay when every hotel in town was booked, brought a birthday cake in the shape of a princess castle.

Just more confirmation for his breaking heart.

"Brianna. You're the person I need to talk to about cookies for the children's ward." Lucy flashed her sweet, dimpled smile.

It didn't even have to be aimed at him for him to fall more deeply in love with her. He was one pathetic sap, he told himself. He needed to man up, put those walls up around his heart and go back to how he used to be—closed off and growly. He put on his best scowl.

"I might as well give you my order while I'm here. I was going to call you, but we are running out of days before Christmas."

"It's coming fast," Brianna agreed with a bob of her head. She was young—still in college—and one of those positive types too. "Haven't you gotten your Christmas shopping done, Spence?"

He scowled harder.

"He's suffering from mall overstimulation," Lucy explained as she looked through her disorganized purse and pulled out what he assumed was the bakery order and handed it over. "The toy store put him in the red zone, but the carolers at the mall nudged him over the edge."

"How many times in a row do they have to sing 'Rudolph the Red-Nosed Reindeer'?" He wasn't upset, but it was a good alibi, and he knew it would make Lucy laugh. He loved her laugh.

She didn't disappoint him. "This coming from Santa Claus. Spence is going to dress up for the hospital kids. Isn't that a kick?"

"Are you sure that's a good idea?" Brianna seemed uncertain.

"I know. You think he would scare the kids, but they loved him." She slipped her hand in his.

How he let it happen, he didn't know. Suddenly her hand was a welcoming presence against his palm, and then suddenly, their fingers entwined, and her peace wrapped about him like hope he could not believe in.

What was happening to him? There was nothing and no one else in his world but her. She was beauty. Her golden hair was storm-tousled, and her creamy complexion was pink from the snow and—just perhaps—because of him. Her emerald eyes shone as if full of dreams. She made the edges of his hard heart weak.

She was a dreamer. He was a man who didn't believe in dreams. A wise man would get out before he got hurt.

"I'll have a fudge chocolate monster muffin." He gave his order crisply, the way the old him would have done it. He kept his scowl in place and added the Eye.

"Good idea," Lucy seconded. "I'll have one, too. And two cups of peppermint tea to go."

He meant to scowl even harder, but he didn't think it worked. Lucy was unfazed, and Brianna rang up the total.

He hauled out his wallet and tossed a twenty on the counter. "Keep the change."

"Thanks, Spence." Brianna smiled.

He knew she was putting herself through college. A few extra bucks would help her out.

"You are marshmallow fluff, Spence McKaslin," Lucy accused him the second they were out of the shop with bags in hand. "You gave her a ten-dollar tip."

"I want to encourage her to stay working for Ava. If she doesn't make enough money here, she may try to hit me up for a job."

"A likely story." She wasn't fooled. She crunched through the snow to his truck. "I hadn't realized there were more of you McKaslins in this town."

"Sure. Brianna's sister is one of Danielle's new hires." Spence opened her door.

He was such a gentleman in the little things and the big ones. He was such a good man. He made her dreams alive again. Standing close to him, she could see what it would be like to be his wife, to be tenderly and respectfully loved by him through every day of every year of her life to come.

Please, let him love me too, she prayed. Her hand found his, and he boosted her up; she felt airborne. She settled on the seat, but her spirit was still weightless.

She loved him so much that there was no way to measure it. For a moment, she thought she saw the same in his eyes. His free hand caressed the side of her face with a touch more gentle than she had ever known. He said nothing while he stood there, gazing at her.

Was it sadness she felt in the air between them? He pulled away before she could be sure. He tugged the seat belt free for her and then closed the door. She felt safe and snug watching him circle around the front of the truck. He looked good—too good. Her heart ached with secret love. Her spirit brightened when he flashed those dimples of his. Her soul felt bigger, lighter as he opened the door and settled behind the wheel.

"We lucked out. Look at that." Spence nodded toward the windshield.

Brianna was turning over the sign hanging in the door. The flashing twinkle lights winked out. The Christmas tree in the corner went dark.

"Something tells me they would have stayed open a few more minutes for you." She winked at him.

"True, but I didn't want to make them stay open any longer. It's starting to snow again."

"It is." Tiny, perfect flakes tumbled from a velvet black sky. She thought of how everything broken in her life was healing, how everything she thought lost was found. She was grateful to God and to Spence. The man beside her was scowling again, but nothing could chase the joy from her heart.

Like those perfect pure bits of snow, she could see

her dreams taking shape: falling in love with Spence more every day, a small intimate wedding ceremony with family and close friends, a baby a few years after that. Tenderness nearly drowned her. She felt too full of happiness to breathe. Those impossible dreams of happily ever after, of true love and family were possible now because of Spence.

He leaned close and kissed her cheek. Sweet and gallant, she thought, but when he spoke, she wasn't so sure.

"I'll drop you off at your car." He started the engine and checked his mirrors before he shifted into Reverse. "It's getting late."

"It is." It was after nine o'clock. And she still had work waiting for her at home. She didn't regret all the time she spent shopping for the kids tonight or with Spence. Although the precious moments had already passed, they would remain forever as beloved memories. "I suppose you have to be to work early in the morning."

"You know it. My boss is one of those workaholics."

"Mine, too." She laughed lightly. "I have a deadline at the end of the month, but I want to get the book out before I head off to Portland."

"How long will you be gone?"

"Just a few days. I want to spend time with my family. We might not see eye to eye, but I love them."

He was sure they loved her, too. "I'm sorry you're distant from them."

"Me, too, but you can't change some people. Just like they can't change me."

"Yes, I know exactly what you mean." He thought of Linda, who had done her best to be a good wife and mother. He believed that—she just wasn't the giving type nor was she kind. The little boy he had once been would have wanted to change her leaving, to have made everything right so they could have somehow tried to find a way to be a happy family.

But the truth was, Linda's leaving was the best thing that could have happened. It brought them Dorrie, a woman who did love them unconditionally. Dorrie was a mom who knew how to stay and love and be kind. "I'm never going to be an optimistic person."

"That's what I like about you, Spence. You might be a scrooge, but you're a scrooge in a Santa suit."

There was her optimism, trying to paint him in a better light. He pulled across the street and into the shopping center's parking lot. The stores were going dark, and the parking lot was emptying out, kind of the way he felt. "I'm not what you think I am, Lucy."

"Are you telling me you're not a grinch anymore?"

"No, the spirit of the season didn't change me." He was going to disappoint her. It was only a matter of time. He may as well do it now. He pulled to a stop at the curb next to her apple-green, impractical car. The truth was tearing him apart. He felt raw from head to toe. "I see how you look at me."

"You do?" Vulnerable, her wide eyes watched him, so intensely green a man could lose himself forever in those emerald depths.

"It's how I feel about you, too. But Lucy—" He stopped, praying for the courage to do the right thing. "All I see is heartache for both of us."

"How do you mean that?" Sadness pinched her lovely features, and he died a little inside.

Had she been doing that thing women did? Starting to dream, picturing the wedding, seeing her fairy-tale future? He hated that he had put this off. He hated that he could no longer avoid the simple truth, the truth she could see if she wasn't a dreamer. "I can't deny that I feel something for you, but I have to be honest. The last thing I want to do is h-hurt you."

"I see." It was too late. Hurt welled in her eyes and filled the air between them.

He steeled his chest, determined not to feel a thing. It was safer that way. Sensible. Smarter. "I am in love with you, but I can't see you anymore."

"What? You're in l-love with me?" She blinked, her forehead scrunched with confusion. "And you don't want to see me?"

"It's for the best, believe me." He ran his fingers through his hair. "I don't believe in love."

"But you just said—"

"I know." He cut her off, not harsh, not gentle either. Pain lined his face. "I don't believe in it for myself. It's never worked out for me. I'm not the kind of man who is good with feelings. I've been like this as long as I can remember. I'll disappoint you, Lucy. A woman like you can't be happy with me."

"What exactly does that mean? What kind of woman do you think I am?" All this time together, and he didn't know? His words were hurting her, but this sliced her in two. "I know what you're thinking. That I'm going to be the one to disappoint you."

"No, never you, Lucy." He bowed his head and closed his eyes for a second, either praying or gathering strength. "I have to admit I thought that at first. I thought you were like Linda, chasing after dreams of fame. But I know you now. I see everything about you. You love so much, you love even when there is no hope. You give freely of your time and your heart. You love everyone. You are like the sun at noon and I am like a moonless sky at midnight. I will make you unhappy."

"I don't understand." Her dreams were slipping away.

Gone was the happy life with Spence. Gone was the family, the wedding, the sweetness of finding true love, all popping like too-full balloons. She was left with the shards of them, needle-sharp.

"I can't be the man you need, Lucy." The pain clouding his eyes was real. He truly believed this. "Believe me, I want nothing more than to love you the way you deserve to be loved. With all a man's heart and soul. With everything he has."

That was how she wanted Spence to love her. It was her prayer now, even as she saw the truth. He would not love her like that. She had pushed him by taking him to the hospital. She had convinced herself that she had seen a deeper side to Spence McKaslin, but that wasn't right at all. No, what she had seen was him doing his best in a situation, that was all. He had been trying, he really had, but it was not who he was down deep. She had been wrong.

Maybe that hurt the most. She drew in a gasp of air, trying not to let him know. Her spirit felt crushed, her soul nothing but fragments. Her heart without his love would never be the same.

"I can't give you what I don't have." Spence sounded broken, too. "It's killing me, because I want—" He rubbed the back of his neck, gazing off at the dark store sign in the window in front of them. "I want a life with you. But I'm not enough, Lucy. I don't have a heart to give you."

Tears scorched her eyes. She popped open the door, desperate for some fresh air. As the cold wind pummeled her and snowflakes beat against her coat sleeve, she saw that he was hurting, too. The shadows had returned to his eyes, darkening them, darkening him.

"Do you understand me, Lucy?" His bark was more plea. His grimace was entwined with defeat.

He was telling the truth. Shock battered her. Disappointment left nothing of her dreams but smoke and ashes. Her throat burned with unshed tears, but she was able to force out words. "You don't want me."

"No, that isn't it at all." Agony twisted across his handsome face. "You shouldn't want me. I'm doing the right thing for both of us."

"The right thing? How can you say that?" Snow needled her face; at least she was sure it was snow. "You aren't even going to try, are you? You say you don't have any heart, but that's not true. I saw it, Spence. I know who you are down deep."

"You're wrong, Lucy. You can't put me in a Santa suit and expect a miraculous change. I know that's what this was about. You've been very straightforward about it. I have to give you credit for honesty. But the spirit of the season is not going to change me. You can't change me."

"No, only you can do that. You're right." Maybe she was seeing the very last bit of Spence McKaslin, the part he kept carefully concealed all this time—the bitter man who refused to accept love.

Anger rolled through her. He could just let true love slip away? A rare and blessed gift that only came around maybe once in a person's life. That meant that it was nothing to him. That she was nothing to him.

"Fine. You win." She slid to the ground. "I'm out of your life."

"Lucy, you're upset."

"That's not surprising, and you know it." She drew her things to her. "You kissed me, Spence. You made me think—" *that you loved me.* Her voice threatened to break, so she didn't say it. She couldn't.

"Lucy, I'm doing the responsible thing here. You will see that in time. I don't want to mislead you."

As if the kisses hadn't done that? As if his tenderness and loving care hadn't roped her heart to his? She understood this man too well. This had happened to her before. She snatched the cup of tea from the holder. The cup singed her fingertips, but she hardly felt it. What she did feel was his hopelessness. It crept toward her like darkness, one bleak inch at a time.

"You will see that I'm right." He tried to reassure her or perhaps it was himself he was trying to reason with.

"If that's what you believe, then I'm sure you are right. I don't want a man who doesn't want me more than his own life. Life is too short, and love is too important." With her soul aching and her battered heart in hand, she shut the door.

Her last image of Spence was of the big loner of a man sitting military straight behind the wheel, tortured with pain and shrouded by darkness, by a heart that refused to accept love.

I can't give you what I don't have. His words thundered through her head. She had been wrong to trust him. He had disappointed her. Worse, he had broken her heart. There was nothing left to do but leave.

Agony kicked through her like a migraine setting in. She ripped her gaze from his. As she headed straight for her car, wetness streaked across her cheeks. She hoped it was snow, because she did not want it to be tears.

He couldn't go home. He couldn't face the loneliness that was without end. If he couldn't trust Lucy, then he couldn't trust anyone. It was that simple. He didn't know how to get past the panic and the doubts. Even if he could, then that still left one truth too painful to face. So he drove through the storm to Rebecca's condo, first, glad he still had the snow shovel in the back of his truck, from when he had first shoveled out Lucy's car.

Remembering made him smile and warmed the icy places within him. Man, he was a fool. He had broken off things with the only woman he would ever love. He didn't need to be able to see into the future to know that. He'd done the right thing. It was best to take this hit now rather than take a bigger one later, when he was even more in love with her. It was better to play it safe than to have the unavoidable truth rise up to destroy him. Because that's what it would do to him when Lucy figured out that she couldn't really love him. No one could. It was just a fact.

He swung into the condominium complex where Rebecca lived. Snow was really coming down now, but when he pulled to a stop in front of his baby sister's walkway, it had been recently shoveled. The front blinds were closed, but light blazed behind the slats. Chad had probably walked over to clear her walk, and the two lovebirds were probably sharing a cup of hot chocolate.

Good. He was glad for the two of them. Rebecca had found a dependable man to love her. That's what mattered. Rebecca was a great kid; she deserved the kind of man who looked out for her and who took her care seriously. Spence nodded approval and swung his truck around. There was no sense heading up the hill to Ava and Brice's ritzy house. They had a company come to regularly remove their snow. Aubrey and William lived over an hour's drive from town in the mountains. William had a plow attachment for his truck to clear his mile-long driveway.

When he turned onto Danielle's street, he could see all the outside lights shining down on Jonas, shoveling the walkway while that silly dog they'd adopted ran in circles, frolicking in the snow. Spence thanked the good Lord that Jonas was able to take complete care of his family again and tried not to feel hurt that he was no longer needed. He turned the truck around in the intersection. Normally he would stop by and visit for a while, but he was hurting too sorely and Dani, bless her, would notice and try to figure out why.

As he drove through the town streets decorated with bright Christmas stars and flashing candy canes and silver bells, he thought of past Christmases. He thought of the wonder and grace of the church service, of the excitement of the mounds of gifts beneath the decorated tree, of the delicious aroma of a ham baking while Dorrie puttered in the kitchen, happy knowing that they were all together, a family.

The trip out to his grandmother's was dicey, and he did everything he could to keep Lucy out of his mind. He refused to let a single image into his head of her little green car trying to navigate country roads. What if she was having trouble? He resisted the urge to call her and see if she had reached home safely. What was wrong with him that he couldn't turn off his worry and his love for her and go about his life like business as usual? He was pathetic, that's what. Only a weak man could not control the direction and tides of his heart.

He pulled into Gran's driveway. Her house was dark. She was an early-to-bed, early-to-rise sort of lady. The driveway was already neatly plowed and the walkway carefully shoveled and deiced. Caleb, Spence realized, Lauren's husband, must have just finished up. They lived up the road. Turning his truck around, he headed for home.

Katherine's driveway was unshoveled. Finally. He pulled to a stop at the curb and realized the house was dark. Not a single light shone anywhere. If he squinted, he could just make out a set of tire tracks from the garage door to the road, filling up with snow.

A bad feeling crawled through his stomach. If something was wrong, he thought, then someone in his family would have called him, except for the fact that he had turned off his cell hours ago. He hadn't wanted any of his sisters calling him and realizing that he was out with Lucy.

He jabbed on the power and waited what felt like one hundred and two years before the phone was functional. He scrolled to his messages. He had twelve voice mails. He hit Call, his heart pounding as he pulled the truck away from the curb.

"It's me, honey." Dorrie's voice sounded strained. "Katherine's on her way to the hospital. Jack's riding in the ambulance with her. I'm going to take Hayden with me to the emergency room. You'll meet us there?"

Ambulance? He turned to stone. Fear beat with enough force to break granite. He listened, driving on autopilot. There was a beep and another voice. This time it was Danielle's. "Spence? I'm heading for the hospital now. I thought you would want to know that Katherine is being prepped for surgery. I don't know how bad it is, but they are afraid for the baby. Call me when you get this."

The beep that ended the message felt like a final tone from a heart monitor. He checked the time. Dani's call had come less than an hour ago. Surely everything was okay, right? He couldn't stand to listen to the rest of the messages. He hit Dani's cell number and nearly drove through a red light.

He hit the brakes, slid to a stop and drew in a shaky breath. He had to calm down. Tonight had been one bummer of a night. He prayed it wasn't about to get worse.

Chapter Fifteen

"Here you are, Dorrie." Lucy set tea on the end table in the small waiting room. "The cafeteria had limited choices."

"It's fine, dear, don't you worry." Dorrie sniffed, somber and teary-eyed. "It's something hot to soothe my nerves. Thank you for fetching this for me. It was good of you to come."

"Danielle called, so I came. It's that simple." Lucy had been halfway home fighting the roads and tears when her cell phone rang. She eased into a chair on the end row next to Dani. "Katherine is a good friend to me. Of course I had to come."

Most of the family had shown up. From Gran to Rebecca's fiancé, Chad. Aubrey and William were still on the road. Only Spence was missing.

"It's been so long. Why haven't we heard?" Dorrie toyed with the tea bag. "Something's gone wrong, I know it. Katherine was not in good shape. My poor little girl. I hate sitting here. I can't do a thing for her."

At her side, John McKaslin slipped his arm around her shoulder and drew her to his strong chest. "Jack promised to tell us the minute he has any news. All we can do is wait and pray. That's what Katherine needs right now. Our prayers."

"You're right, John. Look at me. I'm falling to pieces."

"I'm right here with you, sweetheart." He kissed his wife's cheek tenderly.

Lucy melted. Sweet, true love: What could be more important? She wrote about it in the quiet of her study, tapping out happily ever afters through long daily stretches of lonely work. True love was her dream and her only Christmas wish. It was impossible now.

She thought of Spence and how he had driven away the moment she had gotten her car started, as if eager to be rid of her. She had not imagined his feelings. He simply hadn't felt as strongly—certainly not strongly enough to overcome what haunted him. Sadness crashed through her with tidal wave force.

Don't think about it, Lucy. She banished all thoughts of Spence from her mind. She had to hold it together until she was home alone. She would not fall apart in front of his family. Her heart was shattered, but her sadness was nothing when compared to the reason they were gathered here, waiting for news. Katherine's welfare and her baby's life were paramount.

"Spence!" Dorrie's face lit. "There you are. I was just starting to worry about you, too."

"No need to worry about me." Spence strode into the room, a mountain of a man dusted with melting snow. His face was granite, his jaw clenched, his hands fisted. "Katherine? The baby?"

"No word."

Dorrie's voice sounded far away, as if from a distance. Lucy kept her head low, fighting not to look at the man who had coldly rejected her an hour ago. His words kept replaying in her head. I don't have a heart to give you. *The spirit of the season is not going to change me. You can't change me.*

But I have already given my heart to you, she thought, hating that her gaze went to him, always to him, against her will, against all hope. He looked like strength and decency and everything good in a man as he sank into an empty chair and buried his face in his hands. He sat still as iron. He didn't even appear to be breathing.

Nor was he aware that she was in the room. Ouch. She released a deep, slow breath, letting the pain escape. The waiting room now felt too small. Spence's presence seemed to be shrinking it, and seeing him was like looking at another wedding she wouldn't have, another love she would never know, a family she would be forever without.

She grabbed her coat and her bag and stood.

"No, don't go." Danielle's whisper came quietly. "He needs you to stay."

"He? You mean Spence?" She remembered the man who had kissed her with untold gentleness, the man who now seemed a stranger. "No, he doesn't need me. He never will. I came for Katherine."

"Then stay for Katherine."

"I'll head down to pray." Serious prayer seemed to be in order for all that had gone wrong this day. "Please call me if you hear any news."

"Of course." Tears stood in Danielle's eyes. Maybe it was her fear for her sisters or maybe her brother.

Lucy, unable to say what she felt, slipped down the aisle. She nodded to Dorrie, John, Ava and Brice as she passed. Rebecca lifted an eyebrow in a silent question.

"Chapel," Lucy whispered, not to disturb Lauren and Caleb, who were broth praying.

She had reached the last chair where the big man didn't move. She felt him watching her as she slipped past. Her soul cracked into tiny bits as she walked away from him. What she would give if he would have reached out to her and told her that he needed her. She wanted nothing more than for Spence to be the man she had fallen in love with.

But he wasn't. She stood in the wide archway with her back to the corridor for one final look at him. For all his strength and outwardly giving nature, he was a scrooge at heart. Everyone had been right about that. He had not truly loved her.

If only she could say the same. She padded into the long, empty corridor, feeling every step she took away from him. Loneliness wrapped around her. Bleakness filled her. All hope was gone, but not her love for him. No, that remained like a bright beacon that would not fail.

She acknowledged that it was a cruel twist of irony as she walked the echoing hallway, more alone than she had ever been.

"Spence, are you all right?" Rebecca slipped into the chair beside him and sidled up close enough that her shoulder bumped his, an act of comfort.

He stiffened. He didn't accept comfort, not even from his family. "I'm worried about Katherine and her baby."

"You're taking this awful hard. Don't get me wrong, I'm scared. But this is a really good hospital, and she has the best doctor in town. I know with God's help they are doing everything they can for her and the baby."

Rebecca's hand settled on his midback, another act of comfort from little sister to big brother.

He shrugged away from her. He didn't need anyone or anything. Really, he didn't. He especially didn't need to walk in here and see Lucy Chapin sitting with his family. Or to watch her leave because he came into the room. The look on her face—

He screwed his eyes shut, fighting to keep from seeing the bleak misery on her face.

He'd done that to the only woman he had ever loved, to the woman he loved more than his life and with everything he had. He had wanted to reach out to her, but how? Even if he could figure that out, he had blown it with her. She probably hated him. He didn't blame her. He pretty much felt that way, too.

"Jack." Dorrie was already on her feet and rushing across the room.

"Katherine's fine. The baby's fine." Jack looked exhausted as he held out his arms and wrapped Dorrie in them. Dorrie's sobs of relief filled the room. "Our son weighs nine pounds, two ounces. They tell me he's perfect."

Everyone gathered around Jack. The sisters asked questions. What color is his hair? Who does he look like?

Spence felt frozen in place. His anxiety for Katherine hadn't left him. He felt more tied up than ever. His chest felt so constricted that he wasn't sure if he would ever breathe normally again. This wasn't the way it was supposed to be. He ought to be able to feel happy about this, to feel relieved, to feel something, anything, besides the suffocating grief on Lucy's face.

He had hurt her more than he'd ever intended. And why? That's what he didn't get. Sure, he was hurting as if someone had taken a fireman's ax to his soul, but that was because he was in love with Lucy. Of course ending things with her had hurt. So, why was she in agony?

Because maybe she had really been deeply in love with him. That realization came in a quiet, impossible voice. That was hope talking. That was his deep-seated wish for Lucy to love him; that was all and nothing more. It was his dreams talking, not hers. There was no way that anyone could love him that much.

"Are you all right, son?"

He straightened up, surprised to find his dad seated beside him. "Just a long day."

"It's been quite a worry, but everything is all right. Looks to me like something else might be bothering you." Dad was a kind man, always with little to say but patient when it came to listening.

He recognized that understanding look on his father's face. He squared his shoulders, steeled his chest and did his best not to wonder if Lucy was still in the chapel. "You know me, Dad. Nothing is bothering me that a little hard work won't cure."

"All work makes for a lonely man. I noticed there was something between you and Lucy." Dad was sharper than he appeared. "You've got serious feelings for her."

"What I've got isn't fatal. I'll get over it."

"I was sort of hoping you wouldn't. I got to know Lucy when she was over for Thanksgiving dinner. Dorrie loves her. The girls rave about her. She might have herself quite a career, but she seems like a down-to-earth girl to me. The sort that might make a very good and loyal wife."

"Where did you get an idea like that?"

"The wife part or the down-to-earth part?"

"Neither one matters to me." He didn't know why he

had asked. "I'm a confirmed bachelor. I'm not going to be fooled by a fairy tale."

"You know I love you, son, but you are as stubborn as they come. Dorrie says you get that from me. I don't know about that—"

"I agree. I'm not stubborn." Spence tried to scowl but it came out a little like a grin.

"Me either." Dad's smile was brief. "Let me tell you something. Real love is no fairy tale. Look what Dorrie and I have. It's lasted over twenty years. I'm not saying we haven't had our challenges, but at the end of every day one thing remains the same. I love her. She loves me. We are a team."

"You got lucky with Dorrie."

"How do you know Lucy won't be lucky for you?" Dad cleared his throat, clearly uncomfortable. "Look at the girls. Every one of them has been just as blessed. I can't thank God enough for finding good, true men for my daughters. I pray that you will find someone, too. But you gotta open up. You gotta let someone love you. Just might be that if you do, you'll get exactly what you want. What we've all been praying for."

"I'm happy with the way things are." Spence watched disappointment slide across his dad's face. "Sorry, but don't waste your prayers on me."

"You are my son. Loving you and praying for you will never be a waste. I'm sorry for you. It has been my wish you would have a son one day so you understand how Dorrie and I love you. How much you have been loved all this time." Dad stood. "Looks like everyone's heading off to see the baby. Are you coming?"

He shook his head. His father's words were like bullets embedding deep. *You gotta let someone love you.*

*I'm sorry for you. It has been my wish you would have
a son one day.*

A son. That was a lethal blow.

"C'mon, Spence." Rebecca was at his side. "Don't
you want to see your new nephew?"

"No." He frowned. He wanted to say "yes." But the
truth was, he didn't know how he would handle it right
now. His heart was with Lucy, always Lucy, beautiful,
precious, loving Lucy.

He wanted Lucy more than he wanted life. There was
nothing he wouldn't do for her—provide for her—protect her, take care of her all the days of his life. Simply
thinking of her made joy rush through him like Christmas morning, and he longed for her love with every un-
used corner of his soul.

"I'll wait here. Let everyone else go ahead."

"I don't know what's going on with you, Spence."
Caring, that was Rebecca. "I'm usually pretty good at
interpreting you, but you're like steel. I can't tell anything at all."

Steel, huh? He grimaced. Once he had thought
being stoic and unfeeling was a good thing. Now, he
was no longer sure. He wasn't sure about anything. Everything he thought he knew and believed in seemed
turned around, but he didn't want to be steel, cold and
without life.

"I've got a lot on my mind is all." He took a long
look at his baby sister, all grown up with her soft brown
curls and diamond engagement ring glittering on her
left hand. Chad waited for her patiently at the doorway, ready to take her to the maternity wing just down
the hall. Their wedding was next month. The last sister
would be married.

Where had the time gone? He wasn't sure. The years

kept going by, each one faster and busier than the next. His sisters had found love and life and were starting families. All he had left was loneliness and his fears.

"You go on without me," he said kindly. "Don't worry about me, Becca."

"I can't help it. I don't want to leave you here all alone."

He looked around at the empty chairs and quiet room. He *was* alone. "Chad's waiting for you."

She gave him a sad smile before she rose from the chair. Chad took her hand, and they walked away together, their silence somehow content and their loving bond unmistakable. Spence got to his feet, feeling choked by the emptiness around him and within him.

The hallway offered no relief. Distant sounds echoed down the long stretch of corridor to his right. To his left were the double doors that led into the maternity area, but instead of his feet taking him there, they carried him to the hallway's end, where a large sitting area was tucked into a corner surrounded by windows.

The cold dark night drew him. He stood at the glass, looking past his own reflection to the snow-covered world outside. A lone figure was ambling down the walkway. He recognized that blue goose down coat and matching knit cap and hair the color of sunshine.

Lucy. Tenderness melted him like spring. Peace came to him like heaven's grace. He fisted his hands, steeled his willpower and forced his feet to remain rooted in place. He would not go running after her like some love-struck fool.

She was heading toward the parking lot. Her head was down, her gait careful on the cement. Snow dappled over her. She seemed sad. He remembered how miserable she was when she had passed by him. Guilt assaulted him.

It had been the sensible, rational decision to break things off, he reasoned. It was for the best. One day he would look back and be extremely glad he let her go, right?

Right. If his heart wanted to cry out differently and if his soul felt defeated, then he could ignore that. He could stamp out every bit of feeling, every iota of grief and every last bit of love for her. Life was about hard work and responsibility, not dreams and not love. And if his vision was blurring, then it had nothing to do with Lucy. He was overcome with happiness for Katherine, that was it. Yes, he insisted, stubbornly. Lucy had no effect on him whatsoever.

And so what if he stood watching, to make sure she made it safely to her car? It wasn't because he cared. He was simply doing the right thing. There were criminals in the world, maybe not running rampant in the hospital lot, but it was better to be safe than sorry.

He waited until she had slipped behind the wheel, had settled in and started the engine before he took his first step away. Instead of zipping out of the lot, she laid her arms on the steering wheel and buried her face. He was too far away to see her shoulders shake, but he could sense them. He could feel the tortured fall of each tear.

Chapter Sixteen

Katherine had fallen asleep by the time he'd wandered into her room. It was very late. Jack clapped a hand on his shoulder. "Can you believe it? It all turned out fine."

"You had about a million prayers helping." Spence kept his voice low. There was a hospital bassinet by Katherine's bedside. The baby was quiet, probably sleeping, too. "You sure had all of mine."

"Thanks. I know it will mean a lot to Katherine, too. I need to ask Dorrie something. Do you mind?"

"I'll hold down the fort."

After Jack was gone, he hesitated going outside the door. He hated to disturb Katherine, but he wanted to take a peek at the baby. His boots made faint squeaks on the tile floor as he circled over to the bassinet.

Bundled in blue, the baby was asleep, tiny fists curled, round face relaxed, looking impossibly fragile. Right away he could see Katherine in him. That was her sloping nose and carved chin. Spence melted a little more. He was another little nephew to spoil and protect and play ball with—not now, of course, but in time.

"He looks like Dad, doesn't he?" Katherine's voice rasped, part whisper, part exhaustion.

"Didn't mean to wake you."

"You didn't. I was resting. I can't believe he's here. The last nine months have seemed like forever, and suddenly, here he is. He's too good to be true. But he is."

"Yes, he is." Spence couldn't get Lucy off his mind. The roads were awful. Someone in the family should have offered to take her home. "I'm glad you're both okay."

"We're more than okay. We're all happy. Deliriously, perfectly happy."

That was what he had been praying for, for each of his sisters. He was grateful to God for answering those prayers.

"I want you to meet John Spencer Munroe." Katherine's voice was pure love. "We named him after Dad and you."

"Me?" That was *not* emotion burning behind his eyes. Spence stubbornly blinked, struggling to make his heart stone once again. It was impossible. He used to be in control of his feelings. He used to be stone and steel. And now, look at him, all sappy with feelings. It was Lucy's fault. Lucy, and nobody else.

"Kath, that's real nice of you and Jack."

"You've been a good big brother to me, Spence. You are always there for me if I need you."

"I'm always going to be." It was a given. "You're a pretty great sister, Katherine."

"You're a pretty great brother." Her eyes teared up, letting him know she heard what he couldn't say. "I'm going to rest my eyes a little more."

"I'll sit here until Jack returns." Spence leaned back

in the chair, lost in the shadows, listening to Katherine's breathing slow. The baby started to flail his fists.

"Hey there, John." He whispered, leaning close to get a look at the little fellow. "You don't want to wake your mom. You got a real good one."

The baby's eyes opened and squinted up. He seemed surprised to see another human looking down at him.

"I imagine this is all pretty confusing." He scooted to the edge of the chair and offered the baby his thumb. Perfect, tiny fingers curled around it, holding on tight. "You have come to a very good place."

The baby yawned, so little and dear. Too many feelings to name crashed at the walls of his heart, like a flash flood tearing down a dam, leaving destruction in its wake. Dad's words echoed above the rush. *It has been my wish you would have a son one day.*

This was his future—welcoming nephews and nieces into the world, then going home to his empty house full of unoccupied rooms. There was never going to be his own son, no wife with Lucy's smile, no one and nothing but emptiness. He would grow old that way, grumbling about the profit margin at the store, griping about errands that needed to be done, one long day after another.

His vision blurred. That wasn't how he wanted to spend the days of his life, miserly as if pinching moments like pennies, with no one to share it with. Nothing could be worse than never teaching a son to play basketball or never walking a daughter down the aisle. He couldn't stand to think of a future without the comfort of Lucy's love and Lucy's laughter.

The baby's grip on his thumb tightened. Wide eyes gazed up at him, a little unfocused, and the little guy gave a hiccup. There was so much need in the baby's grip that it tugged at Spence's heart and tore it loose.

A son. He wanted that with all his might. There was only one thing he wanted more: Lucy. Dad had been right. He hadn't let Lucy in. He hadn't let her love him. He had been too afraid. Panic began beating at him, and fear whispered in his soul. It had always been like that. He had always been certain he wasn't lovable. But the truth was, his family loved him. Maybe, just maybe, Lucy could have loved him, too. But he had gone and ruined that. He thought of her crying in the parking lot. Yeah, he had ruined things.

Now what do I do? He bowed his head, reaching out to the Lord. *Do I have a chance to make this right with her?*

When he opened his eyes, there was only silence. No blaring answer from above. No indication heaven had heard him.

"What do you think, John?" he asked the baby.

The infant was no help. John's eyes drifted shut and gradually his fingers loosened. What a nice little guy.

Yep, he wanted one of those. He wanted a lot of things he had been too afraid to hope for. But had the Lord heard him? He sat in the darkness a long while and began to dream, just a little, of what his future could be. He imagined Lucy asleep in a hospital bed and their newborn son snoozing cozily in a bassinet. Tenderness broke him in pieces.

There was only one truth he was left with: the shining, flawless love in his heart, his love for Lucy that nothing in this life could diminish.

That was answer enough.

It had been a tough night, and the morning wasn't looking much better. Lucy waded down her driveway, battling the driving wind and drifting snow. She was so cold that her bones were beginning to freeze. Thanks to the mean winter storm, she found no delight in the falling snow.

She was at the end of her mile-long driveway, but where was her car? Nowhere in sight. Only a white hump. Her poor car. She had parked it here last night, unable to battle the unplowed lane. Next winter she was buying a tank. Or at least one of those Humvee things the Army uses. Too bad she hadn't thought to bring a shovel with her.

Maybe she wasn't in the best mood because she'd hardly slept a wink, thanks to Spence. Nothing had been worse than seeing him sitting in that waiting room like a statue, unaffected and uncaring, acting as if she wasn't even there.

She had been up since four in the morning, pounding out the ending to her book. Unlike Spence, the hero in her story had been able to find his heart. He realized that life meant living and not existing. It meant loving fully, as if loss could never happen. For love and everything good in this world is never truly lost. Love matters, life matters, and kindness matters above all.

If only life was one of her stories. She thought of Spence, and anguish ripped through her like a lightning strike. She hated that she loved him so much. She wished she could stop the tides of affection that ran as vast as the ocean and twice as deep.

The wind gusted, cruelly driving snow into her face. She took another step and sank up past her knees in a drift. Great. She pulled her leg out of the deep snow only to realize the drift had kept her boot.

Super great. Maybe it was a sign from above that she should skip the Project Santa meeting. All the volunteers were meeting for a last-minute check to make sure they were on track, so it was important she showed up. The thought of seeing Spence again made her want to go back home and stay there.

She reached into the snow and hauled up her boot.

Before she could finish pulling it onto her freezing foot, a green pickup lumbered around the corner.

Spence. She lost her balance and her sock hit the snow. The boot dangled from her hand as he rolled to a stop in front of her like a shining knight coming to her rescue.

The window zipped down. "You look a little cold. Need any help?"

Seeing his chiseled handsomeness and his solid goodness made her shatter all over again. "I don't need your help."

"Looks like you need someone's help."

"Not yours." She fumbled with the boot in her hand and somehow wedged it onto her snow-caked sock. What she needed was for him to go away. She needed to get over him. She needed to find a way to stop the endless well of her love for him. What she needed was for him to let joy and love into his heart. The chances of that happening had to be nonexistent.

His door swung open and he hopped down, moving toward her in that confident way of his. Oblivious of the pounding snow, his wide shoulders were braced, his jaw set, his mouth a tight hard line. He ground to a halt in front of her. "Katherine had her baby."

"I heard. Danielle called me late to say that everyone was fine."

He towered over her, as cold as the winter storm. Why was he doing this? Panic pummeled her like the wind. She didn't want to hurt anymore. She didn't want to feel the misery of loving a man who could not love her. Looking at him was killing her. He was every piece of her broken dreams. "Why are you here?"

"We have to talk."

"About the project. I should have seen this coming. You're going to kick me off the committee now, aren't you?"

"Uh—" He swiped the snow from his eyelashes.

"It is the only reasonable solution. I understand why you're doing it." She looked even more sad. "At least most of the work is done. Mostly just the gift wrapping is left."

"I thought we were all getting together tomorrow night and having a wrapping party at my house." Call him confused, but he had a lot on his mind. He gathered up his courage, prepared for rejection and tugged the ring box from his coat pocket.

"Don't forget the final catering approval," she went on, talking fast, as if she couldn't wait to get this done with and get far away from him. Or, he realized, maybe she was still hurting something fierce. "Someone has to get any last-minute gifts, if there's an admission on Christmas day."

"Slow down, Lucy." Kindly, he said the words. Gently, he took her left hand and tugged her glove off.

"What?" Her eyes widened when she saw the ring. It was a flawless, two carat diamond surrounded by the finest sapphires money could buy.

Terror hit him like an avalanche, but he held his ground. He steeled his courage and slid the ring onto her finger. "I'm sorry for how I treated you, Lucy. But I promise it won't happen again. I don't know if you can love me, but I love you. Deeply. Truly. Forever. I am and always will be committed to you. Will you marry me?"

"You're proposing to me?"

"You look shocked. It's all right, darlin'." He pressed a kiss to her ring finger. "Do you want me to say all that again?"

"No, I just can't believe it." Tears filled her eyes. "But you said—"

"I know what I said. I used to be a man who was a whole lot more sensible. Now look at me. Kneeling in the snow. Proposing. Blowing an entire certificate of deposit on an engagement ring."

"What will people think?" Happy tears spilled down her cheeks. "You might lose your edge."

"I'm not worried about that." He climbed to his feet and wiped those tears from her cheeks. He was captivated by her. With the snowflakes sparkling in her hair like rare jewels, she made him believe in love. She had changed his world. Yep, it was all her fault, and he thanked her for it. "What I'm worried about is spending my whole life without you. I trust you, Lucy. I believe in you. I need you. My world has no meaning unless you love me."

"I do love you, Spence." More tears. He kissed them away, tenderly, lovingly, just like her Christmas wish come true.

"But you said you can't give me what I want. That you didn't have heart enough."

"Your love changed my heart, Lucy."

She could see that was true. "Your love has changed mine, too."

Sweetness filled her. Joy brimmed over. Her dreams became whole, her soul buoyant with hope. Spence did look changed. There was no more scowl, no more bark, no more bite. He towered over her, more handsome for his open heart. Stalwart, he looked every inch of a man a woman could trust with all her most precious dreams.

Wishes bubbled to the surface: quiet, unspoken hopes for a future with Spence. She saw a lasting, deep true love and children of their own. She dreamed of a long lifetime of little moments spent with her husband, laughing and talking and experiencing life together.

"Yes, Spence, I would love to marry you. How does a Valentine's Day wedding sound?"

"Perfect."

He sounded like a man who believed in love and happily ever afters. He looked like a man who was deeply, endlessly, hopelessly in love with her. She knew, because that was how she felt. Her dreams were coming true. "Do you know what? This is a happy ending."

"I've changed my mind. I like fairy-tale endings." His kiss was tender perfection and full of love without end.

Epilogue

December, three years later.

Gran's kitchen was warm from all three ovens baking away and fragrant with the delicious scents of vanilla and gingerbread and sugar icing. Lucy breathed in the amazing aroma, one that had come to remind her of the best the Christmas season had to offer.

"And then the moose refused to get out of our driveway. He beat his head against the side of the truck until Spence threw food out the window." She recounted the morning's adventure as she carefully braided together strips of plain and red-dyed cookie dough. "I don't know if M&Ms are good for a moose, but he was satisfied. He moved over enough so that Spence could navigate around him."

"I'm glad, because we wouldn't want a moose blockade to keep you from our annual cookie bake-a-thon." Ava stopped squeezing her pastry cone to glance across the room where her daughter, Sierra, was playing with Aubrey's daughter, Lily. The toddlers were busy pushing chunky plastic trucks around on the floor.

"No!" Johnny, Katherine's boy, stood with his hands on his hips, frowning. Apparently the girls did not play trucks to his satisfaction. He grabbed a dump truck and dropped to his knees to show them how it was done.

A baby's cry came from upstairs.

"Looks like Madeline is up from her nap." Katherine shone like the new mother she was—for the second time. She set down the sprinkles, her attention riveted to the stairs. "Spence is up there alone with the babies. Do you think he can handle more than one at a time?"

"Are you kidding? He's excellent at multitasking." Lucy did her best not to sigh. Her opinion of her husband was very high. They had been married just shy of three years. Every day that had passed had been nothing short of magnificent. How could it be anything less? Spence's love, tender and stalwart, made her life ideal.

"You look like a very happy woman." Gran looked up from one of two mixers on the counter and reached for the almond flavoring. "I had my doubts he would ever wise up enough to propose to you."

"He's the best." Lucy gave the braided strands a curve at the top and *voilà*—a candy cane cookie. She eased it onto the baking sheet. "Even more, he's a fabulous father."

"We're all very proud of him," Aubrey spoke up from the far end of the counter, where she was adding decorative touches to a cookie tray of Santa Clauses. She was glowing in her fifth month of pregnancy. "I'm grateful he found you, Lucy. Your love changed him."

"Oh, maybe. I think God was the one who helped him change, but one thing is for sure. He now carries Christmas in his heart every day." She braided another candy cane, thinking of her beloved husband. He was her rock, her shelter, her bliss.

"We can't call him Ebenezer anymore." Rebecca, in her ninth month, could barely reach the bowl of crushed candy canes set back on the counter.

"He's gotten so mellow. We can't tease him about anything." Ava made a face, adorable as always. "I'm totally bummed."

"I'm sure the tradition will carry on," Dorrie spoke up as she scraped creamed butter and powdered sugar from the blender's beaters with a spatula. "It's all part of the circle of life. Little Johnny looks like a Spencer in the making."

"He does have Spence's scowl," Katherine agreed with a laugh as she carried the full sheet of cookies to the stack of ovens. "I'm sure Madeline will have many enjoyable hours in the years to come teasing her very serious big brother."

They all turned to consider the little boy, naturally in charge. He was a cutie enjoying the role of bossing his younger cousins around.

The back door opened and a Dalmatian burst into the kitchen, nails clicking on the floor, nose in the air sniffing as if in rapture.

"Mom!" Tyler trudged into the room heading straight for Danielle, his brown hair tousled, his face reddened from playing in the snow. Madison, with snow caught in adorable brown curls, tapped in his wake. "Mom! We're awwwwful hungry. Lucky's awful hungry, too."

Lucky barked in hearty agreement.

Danielle looked helplessly at the three little ones huddling around her and handed down some warm gingerbread men. "All right. You may each have just one, but you'll spoil your dinner."

Lucky barked, his happy tail beating against the cabinets.

"Thanks, Mom!" The kids said in unison and raced off to the living room.

Jonas, bringing up the rear, closed the back door, smiling in that easygoing way of his. Healed from his injuries, he looked as strong as ever. In his arms was their toddler, Mary. A cloud of fine baby curls framed her cherub's face.

"Cookie!" she demanded with the sweetest smile.

Danielle complied with a kiss to her daughter's cheek.

"Don't I get one?" Jonas asked, and his chuckle was lost by the commotion of a toddler's shoes thumping into the room. Lauren's little girl, Maya, wandered in, hugging her stuffed bunny. She pointed at the counter, babbling excitedly, her father two paces behind her.

"The men need more cookies." Caleb might have been speaking to the kitchen full of women but his gaze pinned to Lauren, who was manning the ovens. The look they shared was of pure love. True love flourished in this family. "Watching football is hard work."

"We wouldn't want you all to waste away." Lauren fetched a plate from the cabinets. "I'll load this up and bring it out to you all."

"As long as you bring it in person so I can kiss the cook." Caleb scooped his daughter into his arms and carried her back into the living room. Her happy squeals filled the house like Christmas joy.

A squeak of the stairs had Lucy turning toward the hallway. As always, every part of her spirit and every piece of her soul yearned for Spence. He rounded the corner cradling two babies, one in each arm.

"I brought Daniel down, too," Spence spoke first to Ava and then to Katherine. "Madeline wanted to stay with her big sister."

"She adores Hayden." Katherine beamed as she reached toward the cabinets. "I'm going to take a plate of cookies upstairs. It's wonderful having Hayden home on college break. I miss her terribly when she's gone, so I have to spoil her."

The family's chatter continued, but it was all background noise as Spence ambled over. He handed Daniel over to Ava, which left him holding their son—their precious Seth.

"How are my two handsome men doing?" Lucy abandoned the cookie making to give her son a kiss on his chubby cheek.

"The two of us are just about perfect."

"Just about?"

"Only one thing could make it better." These days when Spence smiled, it was full-fledged and with all his heart. He was a man who had become the best of who he could be. The store, which his parents had deeded to him, was flourishing, and he had learned not to work such long hours. He had sold his house to Chad and Rebecca and enjoyed living in the country with all that snow to plow and shovel in the winter. Every year, he dressed up in the Santa suit for the hospital kids. He was a dream, and he made her life a dream come true.

"I know what that one thing is." She went up on tiptoe and kissed her husband. Sweetness filled her, as it always did. Bliss left her as if floating in the air.

"Now my life is perfect." Spence leaned his forehead to hers, a tender connection. The bond between them was flawless.

"Mine, too." It was simply the truth. She had the life she had always dreamed of. She had true love, a comfortable home, a job she loved, a wonderful extended family and a beautiful baby she adored beyond measure.

God had given her so many blessings, and she thanked Him every day.

"I love you so much." She laid her hand on Spence's jaw, incandescent.

"Not as much as I love you." He leaned in for another kiss, cradling their son between them. "Not as much as I will love you tomorrow. Every day, I will love you more."

"No, I will love you more."

They smiled together. How she adored this man, her husband. He made her happy beyond imagining. He made every day feel like Christmas.

"It's starting to snow," Rebecca called out.

They turned together to look out the big picture windows of Gran's old-fashioned kitchen. Tiny, delicate flakes tumbled from a white sky, falling across the wintry world and over the house, as if blessing them all with God's perfect grace.

* * * * *

Dear Reader,

Thank you so much for choosing *His Holiday Heart,* the final book in the third McKaslin series. I hope you enjoyed reading Spence and Lucy's story as much as I did writing it. After getting to know Spence over the course of the other books, it was a challenge finding the right woman for him. I needed someone who would not be easily run off by his gruffness and yet someone tender enough to understand him. I hope you enjoy reading how Lucy captures Spence's lonely heart, and that his search to live a life of kindness and love speaks to your heart, as well.

Please drop by my Web page at www.jillianhart.net for extras on Spence's story and a peek at the next McKaslin series.

Blessings and Merry Christmas.

Jillian Hart

Questions for Discussion

1. What are your first impressions of Spence? When he makes sure Lucy has a place to stay for the night, what does this say about his character?

2. What are your first impressions of Lucy's character? How would you describe her? What are her weaknesses and her strengths?

3. What are the ways that Spence protects his heart? How does he isolate himself from others and from life?

4. What is Lucy's opinion of Spence? How does it change as she comes to know his family and him?

5. How does Spence's view of Lucy change through the story?

6. How is God's leading evident in the story?

7. What role does Project Santa play in Lucy's life? How does it change Spence's?

8. What makes Lucy the right one for Spence? What role does her past experience play? How does her view of him change?

9. How are the themes of family incorporated into this story? The values of Christmas?

10. How does the story handle the themes of forgive-

ness and second chances? Discuss your experiences with both.

11. Spence's miserly heart becomes a holiday heart. What happens to force him to change? What does he realize?

12. What makes Spence take the risk of offering his heart to Lucy?

REQUEST YOUR FREE BOOKS!

2 FREE INSPIRATIONAL NOVELS
PLUS 2
FREE
MYSTERY GIFTS

Love Inspired.
HISTORICAL
INSPIRATIONAL HISTORICAL ROMANCE

YES! Please send me 2 FREE Love Inspired® Historical novels and my 2 FREE mystery gifts (gifts are worth about $10). After receiving them, if I don't wish to receive any more books, I can return the shipping statement marked "cancel." If I don't cancel, I will receive 4 brand-new novels every month and be billed just $4.74 per book in the U.S. or $5.24 per book in Canada. That's a savings of at least 21% off the cover price. It's quite a bargain! Shipping and handling is just 50¢ per book in the U.S. and 75¢ per book in Canada.* I understand that accepting the 2 free books and gifts places me under no obligation to buy anything. I can always return a shipment and cancel at any time. Even if I never buy another book, the two free books and gifts are mine to keep forever.

102/302 IDN F5CY

Name _____ (PLEASE PRINT) _____

Address _____ Apt. # _____

City _____ State/Prov. _____ Zip/Postal Code _____

Signature (if under 18, a parent or guardian must sign) _____

Mail to the Harlequin® Reader Service:
IN U.S.A.: P.O. Box 1867, Buffalo, NY 14240-1867
IN CANADA: P.O. Box 609, Fort Erie, Ontario L2A 5X3

Want to try two free books from another series?
Call 1-800-873-8635 or visit www.ReaderService.com.

* Terms and prices subject to change without notice. Prices do not include applicable taxes. Sales tax applicable in N.Y. Canadian residents will be charged applicable taxes. Offer not valid in Quebec. This offer is limited to one order per household. Not valid for current subscribers to Love Inspired Historical books. All orders subject to credit approval. Credit or debit balances in a customer's account(s) may be offset by any other outstanding balance owed by or to the customer. Please allow 4 to 6 weeks for delivery. Offer available while quantities last.

Your Privacy—The Harlequin® Reader Service is committed to protecting your privacy. Our Privacy Policy is available online at www.ReaderService.com or upon request from the Harlequin Reader Service.

We make a portion of our mailing list available to reputable third parties that offer products we believe may interest you. If you prefer that we not exchange your name with third parties, or if you wish to clarify or modify your communication preferences, please visit us at www.ReaderService.com/consumerschoice or write to us at Harlequin Reader Service Preference Service, P.O. Box 9062, Buffalo, NY 14269. Include your complete name and address.

LIHDIR13R

ReaderService.com

Manage your account online!

- Review your order history
- Manage your payments
- Update your address

---

*We've designed
the Harlequin® Reader Service
website just for you.*

Enjoy all the features!

- Reader excerpts from any series
- Respond to mailings and
  special monthly offers
- Discover new series available to you
- Browse the Bonus Bucks catalog
- Share your feedback

Visit us at:

ReaderService.com

REQUEST YOUR FREE BOOKS!

2 FREE RIVETING INSPIRATIONAL NOVELS
PLUS 2 FREE MYSTERY GIFTS

YES! Please send me 2 FREE Love Inspired® Suspense novels and my 2 FREE mystery gifts (gifts are worth about $10). After receiving them, if I don't wish to receive any more books, I can return the shipping statement marked "cancel." If I don't cancel, I will receive 4 brand-new novels every month and be billed just $4.74 per book in the U.S. or $5.24 per book in Canada. That's a savings of at least 21% off the cover price. It's quite a bargain! Shipping and handling is just 50¢ per book in the U.S. and 75¢ per book in Canada.* I understand that accepting the 2 free books and gifts places me under no obligation to buy anything. I can always return a shipment and cancel at any time. Even if I never buy another book, the two free books and gifts are mine to keep forever.

123/323 IDN F5AN

Name	(PLEASE PRINT)	
Address		Apt. #
City	State/Prov.	Zip/Postal Code

Signature (if under 18, a parent or guardian must sign)